A Fistful of God

Therese M. Travis

This is a work of fiction. Names, characters, places, and incidents either are the product of the author's imagination or are used fictitiously, and any resemblance to actual persons living or dead, business establishments, events, or locales, is entirely coincidental.

A Fistful of God

COPYRIGHT 2012 by Therese M. Travis

All rights reserved. No part of this book may be used or reproduced in any manner whatsoever without written permission of the author or Pelican Ventures, LLC except in the case of brief quotations embodied in critical articles or reviews.

eBook editions are licensed for your personal enjoyment only. eBooks may not be re-sold, copied or given to other people. If you would like to share an eBook edition, please purchase an additional copy for each person you share it with.

Contact Information: titleadmin@pelicanbookgroup.com

Cover Art by *Nicola Martinez*

Watershed Books, a division of Pelican Ventures, LLC
www.pelicanbookgroup.com   PO Box 1738 *Aztec, NM * 87410

Watershed Books praise and splash logo is a trademark of Pelican Ventures, LLC

Publishing History
First Watershed Edition, 2013
Electronic Edition ISBN 978-1-61116-253-0
Print Edition ISBN 978-1-61116-254-7

Published in the United States of America

Dedication

To my four: Heather, Jon, Daniel, and Meg.
You are my greatest joys!

Praise for *Keeper of My Heart*

Rebecca Gresham has built walls so thick around herself no one can reach her...not even God. When handsome Adam McCormick comes to town, he discovers a sensitive caring young woman who wants to break free but can't escape her own prison. This story shows us God's redemptive love and the people he often sends to model it for us.

Tanya Stowe

Rebecca has lost her trust not only in men--but God as well. Then enter stage: Adam, who in their small town living, is unavoidable, especially since she has agreed to work as a receptionist at his veterinary clinic... This was a tender romance that I thoroughly enjoyed right from the start. I loved the way through Adam's prayers and influence, Rebecca's heart is turned back to her Savior. It reminded me of the Bible verse about a cord of three strands is not easily broken. This book is a "Keeper."

JoAnn Carter

1

Even in his sleep, Andy clutched the front of my shirt with his fist. He wasn't two yet, and he hated to be left with a babysitter at bedtime even though he loved to play with me during the day. I wiped sweaty curls off his forehead, and his shudders left over from his tantrum shook me, as if I'd been crying, too. I'd tried to put him down on his bed next to Lucas, his older brother. Andy wouldn't let me. Every time I leaned over the bed, he whimpered and clutched my shirt even tighter. So I carried him back to the living room and whispered into his sleeping ears that everything was OK, that everything would always be OK. And Andy went on sleeping on my lap as though he believed me.

His soft weight filled my heart with a kind of warmth that blankets never had. I stared at the top of his head, at his white-peach scalp. I loved this little kid with a fierce, kill-anyone-who'd-touch-him love. Like a mother, I guess. Like Mrs. Donaldson loved him—right through the stinky diapers and the snot he wiped onto my sleeve. Like a mother.

I went on rocking as much for me as him, for the sweetness of holding something I loved tight against me.

I still hadn't moved by the time the Donaldsons arrived home. Mrs. Donaldson gathered Andy and carried him off to bed. I watched her while Mr.

Donaldson counted out my pay. My arms felt light and empty. Funny how such a small body could be so heavy.

When Mrs. Donaldson came out she asked, "Do you want me to walk you home?"

"No, thanks." I took the wad of bills, which would be more than I charged—it always was—and stepped out. My walk home took me past all of two apartment doors to ours.

"That poor girl," I heard her say to her husband. "Who knows what—"

I slapped the metal railing so it clanged my protest and jammed my key into the lock. But I made myself settle into silence as I opened the door. No sense waking Mom if she was asleep.

Once inside I stumbled and knocked something over. I squinted, waiting for my eyes to adjust. Our apartment is never fully dark. The streetlights wouldn't allow that. Pretty soon I saw potted plants lined up under the living room window, all but the one I'd bumped. I straightened it, and the scent of rosemary clung to my fingers.

"Aidyn?" Mom called.

"Yeah, it's me." Who else would it be?

"What time is it?"

I clenched my jaw. Not this again. Couldn't she turn her head a bit to see the clock? I tiptoed to her door and leaned on the frame. "It's a little after eleven."

"So it's not Thursday yet?"

I turned away. Why should I talk to someone who didn't know what day it was? I wanted to run back to the Donaldsons', but I didn't belong there.

"Don't go yet." Mom sat up, wrapped her arms

around her legs, and started to rock, not slow and gentle like she just wanted to visit, but hard and jerky. I swallowed.

"You have school tomorrow." She didn't say it like a question, so I didn't answer. What could I say? Yeah, I have school. It's the middle of the week, middle of October. They haven't abolished school yet, far as I've heard. But she probably wouldn't understand the sarcasm. I nodded.

"You going to be able to get enough sleep?"

Oh, the concerned parent, now? This was rich. This was the woman who woke me, screaming, stumbling around, falling on her face, six nights out of every seven. And tonight she had to *worry* about me?

"I'm fine," I lied.

She stopped rocking, her fingers plucked at the sheet wound around her legs. I backed farther away.

"Wait," she said. "I quit drinking."

"Yeah, I noticed." No bottles had tripped me in the living room, just plants. No booze puddled on the coffee table or soaked into the matted carpet. She still stank, though, not of vomit, but she had that sour stench of old scotch oozing from her pores.

"Three days," she said.

She must have lost count. She had never, since my father died, gone three days without drinking.

"Good for you," I said. "Enjoy yourself tomorrow."

I bolted for my room. Even though she called my name again, I slammed the door behind me and locked it.

Why had I said that? In just a minute she'd get it, and she'd come in here screaming, tearing me apart. She'd say I had no faith in her. I wouldn't support her.

That it was all my fault she couldn't stop, and I was just going to push her back. So she might as well get herself a drink right now, because she couldn't stand how depressed her only kid made her.

But silence swallowed the apartment. I waited, unmoving, on top of the covers, and listened. The mockingbird that kept me company when I couldn't sleep seemed stuck on three different songs. Usually his repertoire had more variety, but it still sent me to sleep.

The next morning I sat on the cracked plastic seat of the kitchen chair and watched my mother. I hated the last few hours of her sobriety, because all I did was wait for everything to go wrong again. Every time she said anything—*anything*—I'd think, OK, what's that really mean? Do I have another hour, or ten minutes, or what?

She left for work before I left for school, and as she walked out she told me, "Have a wonderful day."

I gaped at her back as she ran down the metal staircase. For a minute there I thought she'd meant it. Really, Mom? A wonderful day? Well, you have a sober day. Oh, yeah, that would have been a great answer.

School that day stretched across a couple of centuries, and each time I thought of Mom, my stomach twisted. Only once did I manage to forget about her, when Jackson, the cutest junior at our school, walked past me and gave me his lopsided grin. My stomach lurched then, too, but it felt good, until I remembered who I was and who he was. A boy like Jackson Killain does not see a girl like Aidyn Pierce. A boy like that does not smile at a girl like me. I'd made a mistake.

And there went my stomach again.

After school, I did my homework, halfheartedly, as usual. Maybe less than halfheartedly. As the time for Mom to get off work crept closer, I watched the clock. *Now* she'd sign out and tell Toni, her boss, good-bye. *Now* she'd throw her purse into the car and start the engine. *Now* she'd grip the steering wheel, clenching her teeth. Would she come home, or stop by the liquor store first? And if she did that, who knew how late it would be before she got home, or if she'd get here at all.

I didn't expect to hear her key in the door a few minutes past five. I nearly threw up when I did.

She pushed her way in. She'd moved the plants before she left for work, so they weren't in any danger, but she lugged several more in her arms, along with her purse and a paper bag.

I hate to see my mom carrying brown paper bags, as if their rough color could disguise the shape of the bottle inside.

She glanced at me, set the pots on the floor, then had to squat as one tipped. She righted it and straightened, all the while guarding that bag. Right. Must have her favorite booze inside. She wouldn't take such care of it otherwise.

"You didn't make dinner, did you?" she asked.

"No." Why should I? She barely eats when she's drinking, and who cares what I eat?

"Good." She set the bag on the table and ripped it open. Smells wafted out, and she unloaded Chinese tangerine chicken, chow mien, and egg rolls. I swallowed.

"Let's eat. I'm starving." She held out a plastic fork for me.

I shook my head. "I'm not hungry."

"Why not?" She stood there holding that stupid fork, frowning at me like she didn't get it. I started to gather my homework, but I knew I couldn't get the papers into a single pile before I lost control. I jumped up and bolted for my room.

"Aidyn."

I turned.

The corners of Mom's eyes pinched and the bags underneath darkened. "Come on. I bought it 'specially for you."

"I said I'm not hungry."

"Chinese is your favorite."

How on earth could she remember that? She'd spent years forgetting me, forgetting everything she could about me. Why pick Chinese food to remember?

I stumbled to my room.

"Aidyn!" she called.

I slammed the door and curled on the bed.

I heard her voice again, saying, "This is Beth." A phone call, then. I wrapped my arms around myself. As tightly as I gripped, I couldn't stop my chest from heaving, couldn't stop the shaking or the tears or the fear. Mom on the phone meant danger, anger, and drunkenness.

She'd start out calm, but as she and her drinking buddy, Joyce, talked, her volume would rise. She'd slur, pause to take a drink, laugh, drool into the mouthpiece.

I pulled the pillow over my head so I wouldn't have to listen as she dragged the both of us back into her gnawing abyss.

A few minutes later, she tapped on my door. "I'm going out for a bit," she said. She sounded nervous.

OK, this was it. Going for the booze. No more waiting.

She pushed open my door and I sat up. "You're not driving, are you?"

She threw me a puzzled look. "Of course I'm driving."

"So tonight when you call me from jail, what am I supposed to do? I'll end up in foster care. They'll put me in a group home. I'm too—" I shouldn't have, I *knew* I shouldn't. The last time I'd smarted off, I'd won myself a split lip, but I said it anyway.

Mom flinched. "I'm not drunk, Aidyn." She didn't add the word "yet," but it hung in the air waiting to be heard. "I'll be home in a couple of hours, OK? Don't let anybody in."

Who would I let in? I didn't have any friends, not that she'd know. I'd lost my best friend almost four years before and had barely talked to anyone my age since.

Shannon, the betrayer, had once been my best friend. Now I still see her at school, but I swear she doesn't see me. She senses me, though, like a black, oppressive presence. She looks at me from the corner of her eyes, but I know guilt blinds her from seeing me head on.

No, I'd just become invisible, in the way of all friendless outcasts. My fault...my mother's fault. Who cared? Fact: you can't see outcasts unless you are one.

After Mom slammed the door on her way out, I crumpled on the couch, telling myself scary stories. Like riding in the car with Mom when she couldn't keep it in one lane. Or what would happen if I answered the door to a police officer and then spent the rest of my life knowing my mother had killed someone with her out-of-control driving. Knowing it was my fault.

I stumbled to the front door and leaned against it, crying. Because you know what? After just three lousy days, I'd started to hope. How stupid is that? I threw my glasses at the wall and slugged myself in the face, trying to beat my hope to death.

I even tried to pray, but I could only get as far as asking, *why*? And I knew He wasn't going to give me an answer.

When I finished my tantrum, I had to find my glasses, straighten the frames, and wash my face. And nothing had gotten any better.

After that I pulled out every towel in the house and spread them on the couch and the floor where she was most likely to puke. If I didn't want the job of picking vomit out of the carpet, I had to protect it before she got sick on it.

Mom walked in a few minutes past nine. She smelled more like stale perfume than booze. Her clear eyes took in the towels and she scowled. "I haven't been drinking."

"OK." I folded one and put it on the coffee table. But the way she watched me made me leave the rest.

"Aidyn, we need to talk."

I said, "OK" again.

She sank to that one bare patch of carpet and reached for another towel, rolled it on her lap and bent over it, like she sheltered something precious. "I went to the church," she said. "They hold AA meetings there."

Alcoholics Anonymous, really?

"It's good. It's really good for me. I think it's going to be…I think." She stopped and met my eyes. "I mean, I can't do it for myself. I know I need…I need help, you know?"

I watched her, frozen.

She went on. "The thing is, it's not guaranteed. I mean, I can't—" She snapped a thread from the towel and twisted it around her fingers. "You're not making this very easy, you know."

"I didn't even say anything!"

She shook her head. I guess even keeping all my thoughts to myself is a sin. "OK, on Saturday afternoons they have meetings. Alateen. I want you to go."

"To a *meeting*?" And what good would that do, besides announce to the last few people in the city who didn't already know that my mother drank?

"Aidyn, this isn't easy. This is the hardest thing I've ever done, I swear. You could at least—" She stopped and put her head in her hands. "Dear God, help me."

Who was she asking? And anyway, what could I do? No matter what, it would be my fault.

And like she knew what the truth was, she told me a lie. "It's not you, Aidyn. It's me. I know that. It's just, you don't know how many times I've told myself, 'Today. Stop drinking today. You can do it,' and then you'd mouth off to me, or I'd start thinking about your dad. The next thing I'd be halfway down the bottle, and I wouldn't even know how I got there." She swallowed, rolled the thread into a ball. "Even if…Aidyn, even if I can't do this, you need to go."

"What? To some meeting where kids sit around and talk about how much they hate drunks?"

Mom jerked, but she met my eyes anyway. "If that's what you need to do, yes."

"Boring." Frightening.

She stood up, and I could tell I'd gotten to her. A fierce, angry triumph filled me, speared through with ribbons of fear. Now what? But I already knew.

Mom rubbed a shaking hand over her sweaty face. "I'm going to Mass on Sunday. I want you to go with me."

Another hit, and this one made me bleed. "It's terminal, isn't it?"

"What?"

"You were at the doctor's a couple days ago. You're gonna die, aren't you?"

"I'm fine."

"How many months have you got?" We'd been through all this with Dad.

Mom sighed. "Sorry to disappoint you, Aidyn, but I'm perfectly healthy."

"He didn't check your liver, did he?"

She swore at me and spun around, her arms flailing, like she needed something to hit. I backed against the wall. "Can't you just—" She stopped, gripped her own shoulders, closed her eyes. "It's not your fault," she said. "I can't deal with this anymore tonight."

Neither of us said good night, but that wasn't a habit with us, anyway.

After I crawled into bed, I heard her through the wall, talking again. She and Joyce could go on for hours, though she usually kept the marathons for Friday night so the hangover wouldn't keep her from work. Toni had threatened to fire her; even I knew that much. But tonight—well, tonight, she needed to talk about her rotten kid.

Joyce could get a lot drunker than Mom before they both passed out. I'd seen it, all those lovely times

Joyce came to our place so Mom wouldn't be leaving me alone and neglecting me. I'd be cleaning up after Mom or covering her with a blanket wherever she'd passed out, and Joyce would manage to slosh another mouthful from the bottle. I could just imagine what I'd find in the morning.

Mom must have had a lot to say about me because the conversation went on and on. Blah, blah, blah.

I didn't ask her to think about me!

It wasn't my fault.

I listened to her voice, the long pauses in between. I hated the pauses most, because at least when she was talking, she couldn't be drinking. But the pauses grew, so many, so long, that I finally cried myself to sleep.

2

Saturday Mom started nagging about the stupid Alateen meeting before I rolled out of bed. I staggered after her to the kitchen and watched her slug down orange juice like it was her favorite scotch.

"It'll help both of us if you go," she said. Crooked strips of sun pierced the closed blinds and stabbed her face. But the dim room shadowed her eyes, and I figured they had to be bleary and swollen. I grabbed the cord and snapped up the blind so light flooded the room.

Mom winced and covered her forehead with her hand. "It's at three this afternoon."

I slammed my glass onto the table and juice sloshed over my hand. "Did you even think I might have something to do then?" I shouted and struggled to lower my voice. "I'm supposed to babysit."

"Aidyn." Mom waited for me to look at her. "I didn't know. You don't need to change your plans. There's always next week."

"What if I've got something next week?"

"You make it sound like I'm forcing you." Mom sighed and shook her head like she thought she could convince me how wrong I was. "You have to be ready for it, or it won't help." She took another drink and her hands shook. She *had* been talking to Joyce last night, and now she had a hangover.

Yeah, and she probably had vodka in that juice.

A Fistful of God

"Just like me." Mom's voice came soft and patient, as though she loved this deep, touching subject and knew I cared just as terribly about it. "If I hadn't been ready to quit, I wouldn't have been able to."

Just like her—she thought I was like *her*? "I don't have anything to quit!"

She raised one eyebrow at me, as though I had no idea what I was talking about.

"I'm not the one who drinks!"

"I know."

"*I'm* not the one who throws up because I drink. *I'm* not the one who forgets stuff like birthdays and promises and field trips and teacher conferences because I drink. *I'm* not the one who pretends to quit and then lies and *lies*." I jumped up and backed away, my fists pressed to my stomach.

"I did quit." Mom stood, too.

I backed farther away. "You're lying."

"When did you think I was drinking?"

"Only last night," I snarled. "Only when you were talking to Joyce. Only when you weren't talking I knew what you were doing."

"I was talking to...I was listening, Aidyn. That was my sponsor."

"Was she drinking, too?"

Mom gasped. "Of course not! I swear. I haven't had a drink since Sunday."

"You're lying!" I flailed my arm, grabbed something, and threw it. Orange juice sprayed my mother and the kitchen. "I hate you!"

She put her hands over her face, and I did the same, cowering, sure last Sunday would happen all over again.

"Oh, dear God," Mom whispered. But I knew she

wasn't talking to me. For once, she was really praying.

I lowered my arms. She slumped against the warped counter, juice dripping off her chin, and she shook. "I don't need this, Aidyn. I'm having enough trouble trying not to drink."

We stared at each other, blame separating us.

"I'm sorry." Mom swallowed. If she went on swallowing her anger, she'd make herself sick. "For what I said, and for Sunday." She looked away.

"I thought you blacked out again."

"I wish I had." She looked up at me then. "Aidyn, I am so sorry."

Her tears mixed with the juice, but she still didn't wipe her face. I grabbed a towel. Too rough, I dragged it across her face until she snapped it away. I didn't care. She must be half drunk already, slobbery, sentimental, maudlin. She took the towel from me and clutched it to her chest. "Did I hit you?"

I shrugged. "You were too drunk to hurt me much."

"You have no idea how sorry I am." She turned, wiping the sticky juice from the table and cabinets. I leaned against the table and watched her.

She tossed the sopping towel in the sink. "I was out of control, and I hurt you, and I'm sorrier than you can imagine."

Mom never talked this way. That meeting must have affected her. That or the booze. Maybe she could hold it better now, but she still had to be drunk.

She pointed to the juice pooled on the edge of the sink and dripping to the floor. "You're out of control, too."

I snorted. "I'm not the one with the hangover."

Something sparked in her eyes. "For once, neither

am I."

"That's 'cause you're already half bombed."

"No, I'm not." She shook her head. "I know I'm shaky. I'm getting rid of years of booze. I can't expect to feel great overnight. But I *am* feeling better."

Something hot and acid crept up my throat. She always said that. She'd stumble through the door, shaking with need, then she'd hug that first glass and say, "This has been the worst day, but I'm feeling better."

Now she held out her arms like she wanted to hug me, too. I purposely flinched, but it didn't work that time. "I'm sorry I hit you, baby. I know you hate me because I didn't love you enough. I'm sorry I was always drunk when you needed me." She gave up reaching for me. "I'm so tired of being sorry."

"I have to get my shower." I turned away, as much to hide my shock as to leave. "And then I have to go to the Donaldsons'." I glanced around. I tried to keep the kitchen clean, though how many times had I spent all my energy cleaning up her mess instead? "If you're so wonderfully sober, maybe it's time you took over the housework."

Mrs. Donaldson opened the door when I knocked. "They're still napping. You can take them to the park after they finish their snack, but be home by five. We're going to my in-laws' for dinner." She made a face, and I laughed. She hated taking her kids there, but it was family so she felt obligated. "My husband should be home by then so you won't have to stay." She bustled off to her room to finish getting ready.

I sat at her kitchen table with my history book. I had to study for a test on Monday, but the words went blurry. I yanked off my glasses and rubbed away the tears.

"Aidyn?" I looked up. Mrs. Donaldson's pale face had gone red. "Is your mother all right?"

I shrugged. "Yeah, sure. Why?" She hated attitude, but I didn't care. Why should I have to tiptoe around *her* feelings, too?

She bit her lip. "Lucas heard you yelling again and it scared him." She watched me for a minute, but I stared at my history text. "You know, if you need to talk, I'm here."

I shrugged.

"It can't be easy with your mother the way—" I jerked my head up and she stopped. "Oh, Aidyn."

Everybody in the apartment building knew about Mom.

She glanced at her watch. "I have to go." She sounded like she had a time bomb ticking off her last minutes. "But I'm usually here when you get home from school." Her face went red, but I was just as mortified.

I said, "OK," and we both knew I'd never confide in her.

By three I had the boys at the park. My watch must have broken. It stayed three o'clock for the longest time, only inching to one minute past, then two, after what seemed like hours of agony.

Mom's meeting started at three. My world would stay riveted to three in the afternoon for the rest of my eternity. What did I know about AA meetings? People introduced themselves, said what they were—the one word that defined them all. I tried to imagine Mom saying, "My name is Beth, and I'm an alcoholic."

My mind could not grasp that last word. I'd never heard her say it, and I'd never said it about her.

Knowing is so different. You can know something and never have to admit it out loud, and that makes it bearable.

Maybe it was easier for Mom to say she was a drunk. Maybe it was easier for her to tell strangers what she was.

If I'd gone to the stupid meeting she wanted me to go to, I'd have ended up having to say practically the same thing. I shook my head. How could I say that about my *mother*? How could I ever admit to that horrible, stinking *shame*?

I tried to move my lips across the words. "My name is Aidyn and my mom—"

Lucas tugged my arm. "What did you say?"

"Nothing." The park, crunchy with leaves and full of Saturday visitors, came into focus. Andy held his arms out for the swing. These kids needed me.

I pushed Andy and wondered if Mom had really gone to that meeting. Maybe she'd gotten too caught up in *being* an alcoholic to tell a bunch of losers she was one.

I yanked Andy out of the swing and onto my back. "Race you!" I yelled to Lucas, and I started around the edge of the playground. I ran away from the voice that accused, *if she's drinking right now, it's because you made her, Aidyn. It's your fault!*

Halfway around the edge I saw them, a bunch of boys from the high school, with Jackson right in the middle. I stopped and Lucas slammed into me. I grabbed his shoulder to keep my balance while he screamed, "I caught you! You're it!"

"We're not playing tag." I set Andy down and pretended to tie his shoe while I watched the boys.

I knew almost all of them. Miguel, the clown, and

Wallis, the best basketball player the high school team has had in years. But I couldn't tear my eyes from Jackson. I tipped my head at a neck-wrenching angle to see him through both my hair and glasses. Jackson, with his ice-blue eyes and straight black hair. Everybody's friend, except mine. He didn't know me, but every other kid in high school got to call him a friend.

My feelings for him proved I was just like any other girl, didn't they? Those eyes, that smile, the one he gave to every person he saw. Not to me. He wouldn't see me, but I responded like a real person. At least he gave me undeniable proof that I was alive, that I could be normal. If only…

"Aidyn, come on," Lucas yelled. He grabbed my hand and jerked, and I landed on my knees. Gritty sand dug into my skin, and I bent my head in pain. I heard the older boys laughing. I tried so hard not to look, but I had to. Jackson stood a little apart and stared at me, his eyes shadowed.

Great. He had noticed me this time; he knew me now. He wouldn't know my name, unless he'd heard Lucas, but he'd know me as the klutz.

He turned and melted into the group, and I finally noticed Lucas. "Did I trouble you?" he asked.

I laughed. Where had he gotten such an old-fashioned way of talking?

He touched my cheek with butterfly-wing-fingers. "Mommy says you're troubled. We say *God bless Aidyn* every night."

I sat down flat on the sand and gaped at him. So Mrs. Donaldson taught these little kids how to pity me. I didn't need it! And if I didn't need the money, I'd quit babysitting. But it wasn't Lucas's fault his mother was a busybody.

After a minute, I pulled my head from my bent arms and took a breath to settle my thoughts. "I'm not troubled. Just don't pull on me like that, OK?" By then Jackson and his friends had disappeared. It didn't matter.

I walked through our apartment door a little after five, and there was dinner on the table, heaping plates of spaghetti smothered in sauce, and salads. Balanced and healthy. Wow. And to round things out, a tumbler of wine at Mom's place matched the cup of milk at mine.

At least we weren't pretending she wasn't drinking anymore.

My stomach knotted but at least I knew what to expect.

Mom finished off that first glass before she even took one bite. I wondered if she'd eat at all, but after she refilled the glass from a pitcher in the fridge, she sat down and motioned me to join her.

"How was your day?" she asked.

I picked at a string of pasta with my fingers.

She took another drink, then a bite. Maybe she thought I wouldn't notice how she'd polished off that first glass. Maybe she thought she could fool me into thinking she had Kool-Aid in there. Maybe she was too far gone to care.

When Mom first started drinking, I saw nothing wrong with it. I was only nine and as miserable as my mother, and I felt so safe when she relaxed and smiled and sometimes laughed. I'd missed her laughter the most since Dad died.

But she never stayed—safe.

Now, she couldn't stop drinking. Her words

slurred. If she tried to walk she'd stagger, and if she dropped something she wouldn't notice until it hit the ground. If I told her she was drunk or asked her to stop, she'd get mad, tell me I was only trying to ruin her good mood.

"Remember we're going to Mass tomorrow," Mom said.

I stared at the stringy pasta in my sauce-stained fingers.

"Aidyn?"

I shrugged.

Another long drink. "Set your alarm. We'll go to the nine o'clock service."

I glared at the glass. "You're going to have a hangover," I told her. "You'll never make it."

Her face went tight. "I'm not drinking."

"What about that?" I pointed.

"It's juice. Did you think I would drink in front of you and lie about it?"

Think? I knew. "Yes."

She blinked. "Yeah, well, maybe last week I would have." She pushed the glass across the table. "Smell it."

"No thanks. You probably got vodka or something like that." I pushed it away, glad to see some slosh onto the table. "If you're up, why don't you wake me? That way I won't end up setting my alarm for nothing."

I ran to my room. No matter how much I hoped, nothing would ever change.

Especially me.

3

Sunday morning I checked the clock as soon as I woke up, and groaned. Not even seven yet. I had more than half an hour to wonder if we were going to Mass or if Mom had blown it the night before and couldn't face the world today.

I stared at the gray light that sneaked through the blinds. I'd left the window open and now the cold seeped in. I'd forgotten my heavy blanket even though the last few nights had been chilly. One more thing I'd screwed up. I couldn't get anything right, and terror struggled in my chest. I told myself that blankets aren't a big deal, and then realized I already knew it. I was scared about Mom. And if Mom had stayed sober, that left me free to panic about Mass.

I used to believe what they told us at church. I used to pray God would make us be just like the Holy Family, because they were three people and my family had three people, and the only difference I could tell was that I was a girl. Only Dad died, and Mom wasn't anything like Mary. And me—well, I wasn't anything good, not like their kid. Still, even after Mom got to being regularly hung over on Sunday mornings, I'd go to Mass. With the church just a few blocks from our apartment, I'd walk. I'd find myself a seat and feel, just for a little while, as though when I got home everything would be OK. After all, I kept praying. God wouldn't tell me no *again*, would He? Only He did. But

I kept going until the Sunday after the Shannon thing.

One night, her parents went to a party, and Shannon came to our apartment. Mom joined us as we hunkered on my bed. Shannon and I each had a soda; Mom had her bottle. She was great, at first, telling us stories that made us howl with laughter. But the stories got scary. Not ghost-and-monster scary, but confusing-scary, and way too grownup for a couple of twelve-year-olds. Rather than stare into Shannon's confused brown eyes, I studied my hands, my ragged cuticles.

Mom's drunkenness froze both of us, and we listened like mute toys plunked down after playtime.

When Mom threw up, Shannon called her parents. I had things cleaned up by the time they came to get her, but I couldn't do a thing about Mom.

At school Shannon told me, "I'm not allowed to be friends with you anymore." She looked like she'd been crying, but she didn't look sorry. Mom scared her, and anyway, *Shannon* had plenty of other friends.

The next Sunday, there I was, sitting in the stiff pew while the church filled, watching people give each other hugs then find a seat and pull out the missalettes or a Rosary for meditation. And then I heard a familiar voice. Shannon's mother said, "No, let's not sit there."

I turned. Shannon's little sister argued with their mom and pointed at the long stretch of empty pew next to me. But the woman just shook her head and dragged the kid to the front of the church.

I got up and walked out. I didn't have any friends left, not even God. Why should I go talk to Him when all He did was ignore me?

Shannon's family probably still went. They were the good kind of people. I bet they'd be really happy to see Mom and me.

I heard Mom bumping around in the bathroom, and my stomach clenched. Then a crash. I pulled the sheet over my head. We weren't going to church after all. I knew that before I even got up, but I'd probably get to do a lot of cleaning.

A few minutes later Mom tugged the sheet out of my fingers. "Come on, Aidyn. You get up earlier than this for school."

Something about her eyes and her voice startled me. She *wanted* to take me.

"Aidyn?"

"What broke?"

"Did that wake you? Sorry. I tossed an old bottle in the trash and missed."

I didn't think she was lying, but I couldn't tell.

"Come on, honey." She stroked my hair as casually as if she did it often. "I don't want to be late."

Of course not. She had her agenda, whatever it was.

But did I want to face Shannon and maybe other kids I knew from school? They'd see me, and they'd see Mom. Would this give them the message that I could do normal things like them, or would anyone notice me at all? I shrugged under the shower, trying to loosen my muscles and answer myself at the same time. I'd gotten too used to my own invisibility.

As I got in Mom's car and tried to buckle the seatbelt, a flashback smacked me into the Fourth of July and Mom driving home that night, drunk. I swallowed. Mom hadn't even known what day it was by that time. We'd gone to my grandmother's, but Mom got into a fight with someone, and we left before my uncle started the fireworks. They'd flashed all over the place, though, little islands of bombs going off around us. Mom started screaming, something about them trying to get us, about getting home before they killed us. It would have been trickier to get us home before *she* killed us. We were all over the road. Once we plowed right through the middle of one poor family's display set up in the middle of the street. I shut my eyes and prayed we wouldn't hit anyone. As far as I could tell, God answered that one, and I went out the next day and checked the fenders for dents and dried blood.

Now I couldn't wrestle that nightmare from my mind.

Freshly-shampooed hair drifted across my cheek. Warm hands curled around mine and snapped the lock. Mom tipped my chin up. "I'm sober, Aidyn. I won't hurt you."

I whispered, "OK," but only so she'd start the car and not read my mind anymore.

The nine o'clock service is the most crowded at our church. I saw a couple of families whose kids I babysit and kids from school. I caught Jackson staring at me from a few pews away and ducked my head. If I'd known he'd be there, I'd never have gone. If I'd known, I'd have come years ago. I wanted to die.

My old Brownie leader, from way back when I still did a few normal things, inched into the pew behind us. She glanced at me, frowning. She must know all about Mom. I bet she wondered why we thought we had the right to be there.

Then I turned and saw Shannon with her mother and the rest of her family.

I jammed my hands between my knees and bent my head. I hoped she hadn't seen me. Did I want to be invisible so she couldn't ignore me anymore? Or did I want her to notice how I ignored her?

I squeezed myself as small as I could and remembered religion classes. Shannon and I had gone together, always. I remembered the frilly First Communion dress my grandmother bought me, and how, even at the old age of seven, I couldn't resist sucking the egg-shaped pearly buttons on the collar. I remembered the sweet flat taste of the Host and how clean I felt after going to Confession. I remembered how I believed that if you went to Confession, you wouldn't even *want* to be bad anymore. My father swung me in circles so my pure white skirt billowed like a bell. He'd been so strong, so loving, not sick at all then. Mom had been sober, too. Why couldn't everything have stayed safe?

Mom touched my arm and motioned me to stand. I remembered how we would stand and sit, how I'd measured the boredom of grown-up voices flowing over my head by the kneeler, and how many times it went up and down. I remembered feeling safe here, so long ago, before Dad got sick. I wanted that safety, the peace it brought, so bad.

When it was time for Communion, nausea pushed against the back of my throat. The wine! They served wine at Mass, real wine. How could Mom say she'd quit drinking when she was coming to a place where they served booze to anyone who wanted it?

I let her get in front of me, and I glared at her back, and when she passed by the Chalice without glancing at it, I remembered. I remembered that it is supposed to be the Blood of Jesus, not a ploy to get drunks to church.

After we knelt in the pew Mom whispered, "We should have gone to Confession first."

Oh, yeah, just like I'd gone before my first Communion.

"Next week," she said. "It's right after the meetings—" She stopped, gave me a quick look. "We'll see. We'll figure it out, won't we?"

We? I bent my head as if I needed to pray really hard, and I knew *we* would not figure anything out.

Just before the closing prayer a woman walked onto the altar, and the priest handed her the microphone. "Hi, I'm Lucy. I want to remind all the teens to come to youth group. We've got big plans for you guys, and everyone is welcome."

I leaned closer to Mom. "This church sure has a lot of meetings."

"Don't they?" She sounded calm, but her hands tightened on the back of the pew.

We barely got outside when I heard someone yell, "Hey, Aidyn!"

I froze. Someone here noticed me? Someone saw me here with my mom and still called out to me? I turned to see who it was and thought that freezing was not enough. Melting into nothing would be better.

Jackson walked toward me. "Aren't you coming to group?"

I opened my mouth. Group? Was that the stupid Alateen meeting or the youth group, or what? Whatever, I hadn't been invited. "No."

He turned, and even though I was kicking myself for being so stupid as to say no, I still watched the way his mouth quirked up on one side and sort of folded over itself on the other. Instead of walking away, he held his hand out to my mom. "Hey, Mrs. Pierce. You better make her come. You're the mom, aren't you?"

This could not be real. Mom had stopped drinking,

and Jackson Killain knew my name, not just my first name but my last. I was delusional.

"Doesn't sound like she wants to go." Mom smiled back at him, and I could see he'd charmed her as much as me.

"Oh, come on." He winked at me. I wanted to hide. I felt like a baby being coaxed out of the sulks. "You gonna let a kid tell you what's good for her?"

Mom made a face. "How long is it?"

"Couple of hours. I'll drive her home if that's a problem. Unless you want to wait. We can even grab seats in the back in case you need to get her earlier than that."

For one moment I determined to go. Jackson wanted me. I didn't care which meeting it was. I wanted to go. I wanted to be one of the normal kids that other people, even popular people like Jackson, wanted to hang around. And this once maybe I wouldn't be the kid leaning against the wall, watching everybody else who already had friends ignore me.

And then I saw Shannon. She stood near the hall watching us, her hand shading her eyes. She dropped her hand and flipped her hair back like she didn't want me to know she'd noticed me at all. But I knew. And just as hard as I'd wanted to go, I now wanted to stay away.

Besides, I didn't want my mom and Jackson arranging me like I was some little kid who hadn't been invited to a birthday party and now needs Mommy to soothe her feelings.

I turned to tell Mom I wanted to go home. She stared at Jackson. Her hand clutched her purse strap over and over, her fingers pacing on the leather. It hit me. She wanted to get away as badly as I did. Only *she* needed a drink. If I let her go, she might forget to come back. I'd end up walking home, and everyone would know why.

"I said I don't want to go." I turned away.

"Why not? We're just regular people, you know." Jackson's mouth had gone tight, and I figured he thought I was a snob or something, and I'd ticked him off. Just as well. He had Shannon, after all.

Instead of going back to her, though, he grabbed my arm and tugged me after him. I yanked away but he laughed. "Come on. I bet your mom has something to do. Just come, OK?"

He had no idea what Mom had to do. No idea. I looked back at her, but she just tipped her head toward him, like everything was fine with her. I bet it was. I wanted to cry, but instead I lifted my chin and pretended I wasn't mad.

When we got to where Shannon waited he started to introduce us, but Shannon said, "We know each other." She looked at me with no expression that I could read on her face. What could she be thinking? She'd gotten rid of me years ago, and now she had to deal with me all over again. I ducked my head.

"You do?" Jackson looked from me to her. His mouth did one of its funny little quirks, like he didn't believe her.

"We used to be best friends," Shannon said. It struck me that I hadn't heard her voice in years, but it sounded the same, or softer, not as hateful as I pretended I always remembered. Jackson made a good buffer.

"So why not now?" Jackson asked. Some buffer. He finally let go of my arm, and I rubbed where he'd gripped it. It burned.

"It just happened," Shannon said. She looked down then up again with a brilliant smile I didn't recognize.

I stared at a poster that proclaimed "Believe!" and tried to get my face where I didn't look as mad as I felt. *It just happened*, huh? She was the one who'd walked away from me. She hadn't bothered to stand up for our friendship, so it was her fault. Hers and Mom's.

"OK," Jackson said, and I knew he was holding back on the questions. He'd ask them later, but he wouldn't ask me. Why would he want my take on it?

We sat in the last row as Jackson had promised Mom, me on one side of him and Shannon on the other. In front of us sat a bunch of kids, and I recognized a few. Wallis and Miguel plopped down in the chairs right in front of me, scooching them over so I was pinned in, then Miguel turned and smacked Jackson's knee.

"You're not playing fair. There you sit with those two cute girls and look what I get." He jerked his thumb at Wallis, who waggled his eyebrows and pretended to be coy. "Didn't your mama teach you to share? C'mere, Shannon. Sit with me."

Shannon gave a glare she must have practiced, and he shrugged. When he winked I jerked my chin down, mad that he'd made fun of me. I am not cute. I look like Mom. We're both short, we have long, thin faces, dark, curly hair, and nice eyes, though I don't suppose anyone notices mine because of my glasses.

Lucy's voice boomed over the PA. "Let's get started."

Miguel turned around, and I straightened, though I didn't look up.

Lucy called a couple of names and people

straggled up. Someone had a guitar, and Lucy had a flute, and they started a song that was so different from what they'd played in church that I had to listen. It had a beat, and kids started clapping to it right away. I tried to find the rhythm, but I saw Shannon lean toward Jackson, whisper something, and glance around him at me. I shoved my hands into my pockets and acted like I'd known all along I was supposed to just listen. Like I'd never expected to belong.

After another song, Lucy started a prayer, something about letting the Spirit guide us and getting centered in Christ. I didn't know what she meant, but I was sure that by the time she got to the "Amen" everyone else there was centered and guided and as holy as they could get without being dead and canonized.

Shannon whispered to Jackson again, and I felt my face burn. She might not have been talking about me, but I felt discussed anyhow.

Lucy hitched herself up onto the edge of the stage and sat facing the rest of us, swinging her legs. "I was thinking the other day," she started, sounding like she was talking to a couple of good friends, totally sincere, "how some people give up on God."

She let that sink in. I wondered if anyone there had ever done that, besides me. *They* were the people who went to church on Sundays. *They* got invited to join this group. When would God ever let *them* down?

"It's like they look around, and say, 'Well, He's not doing it *my* way, so I'll find someone else who will.' You ever figure how smart *that* is?" She waited for the laughter to settle. "But think about it. We figure God isn't doing what we want, so we give up on Him. He, however, never gives up on us. Not for anything. We can run away, tell Him we don't want Him, reject Him over and over, and you know what? He'll still be there every time we take a chance and look. He will never give up on us. He will love us forever." She sounded like she believed this. I watched her, saw the way she smiled. I bet it was true.

For her. For them.

She went on talking like giving up was something you could take back.

"We're the ones who give up." Her voice soft as if she wanted to lead us somewhere, and didn't want to frighten us off. "Miguel and Jennifer are handing out slips of paper and pencils. We're going to write down one thing we've given up on, one thing we've quit trusting God for, and then we'll take them outside and burn them."

Miguel, his hands full of pencils, pulled a face at her. "What if we got more than one thing? What if we got like, twenty?"

Lucy smiled. "Then you get more paper."

Someone else asked, "What're we gonna burn it for?"

"Because these are things we need to let go of. We're offering them up, letting God take over on them again. And our offering will be a sweet smelling sacrifice to God." Now she sounded like the Old Testament.

"Father Tom isn't gonna like this," someone from the front said. "He don't like people lighting no fires on church property."

Lucy answered as soon as everyone stopped laughing. "We're doing it in the barbecue, and Father Tom knows all about it." She took her own slip of paper from Jennifer and bent over it.

"I hope she's using lighter fluid," I mumbled. I didn't think I'd said it loud enough for anyone to hear, but Miguel, settling back on his chair in front of me, laughed. I slid down in my seat and refused to look at him.

I wished I had the guts to put something down on that tiny scrap. I'd need more paper than Miguel if I wrote anything, though.

I wanted to go home.

Miguel turned and caught my eye, just when I was thinking he'd forgotten my stupid comment. He waggled his eyebrows, and I wondered why. Was this a joke? Here I took it seriously, trying to act like I knew what was going on, and it wasn't for real?

I glanced at Jackson. He twirled his pencil and frowned at his paper. Shannon wrote in familiar, curly letters. Maybe Miguel was the only one goofing off.

"I know what Miguel is asking for," Wallis said in the loudest whisper I'd ever heard. "A date with Shannon."

"He should've given that up a long time ago," another boy said.

"Like I said." Wallis looked at Miguel and chortled.

"In your dreams," Shannon muttered.

Jackson laughed and took Shannon's hand.

"I'm not dreaming 'bout Shannon no more." In one motion, Miguel lifted his chair and turned it around so he faced backward and stared at me. I ducked my head and pretended I had to roll the corner of my tiny piece of paper just right.

"Yeah, he's just hoping for a date with anyone."

"Shut up, Wallis," Miguel said without looking at him. "Hey, Jackson, who's your friend?"

Jackson introduced us.

I wanted to fall through the floor. I wanted to go home. I'd rather clean up Mom's soured-booze-scented puke than sit there.

"I see you at school," Wallis said. He leaned on his knee and shouldered Miguel out of the way. "You are one quiet kid, you know that?"

I rolled my eyes. "And you're tall. You know *that*?"

It wasn't all that funny, but the people around us laughed.

"My mama would like you." This time Miguel's voice was quiet, private. "She likes smart girls."

I ignored him. I would not open my mouth again. I'd just walk into it if I did.

"Everybody ready? Let's go." Lucy grabbed a matchbook and led the way.

I scribbled a word on my paper, fast, the three letters slurring together so no one could read them, and squashed it into a pill-sized lump. I wanted this prayer, I wanted a chance to believe again, but if anyone said one more thing to me I'd take off. When I looked up, I saw Shannon and Jackson by the door. Jackson watched me, as though he could wait forever, if that's how long it took me. I hurried past them onto the blacktopped yard, slivered between the building and a chain-link fence. On the other side of the fence drivers slowed as they passed us.

Maybe the others weren't taking this prayer thing seriously because they didn't have to. I knew other kids had alcoholic parents, but they wouldn't be a part of a church group either, especially not one that the most popular kids in school also belonged to. Church groups didn't want kids like me. After all, these kids belonged.

At the far side of the yard two lonely briquettes nestled in the center of a huge barbecue. As Lucy lit them, the chattering stopped. One by one, everybody dropped his or her slip of paper into the flames. I watched as each one made the sign of the cross as the paper curled up, blackened, and became ash.

I waited until last. I wanted to wait until everyone had gone back inside, but Lucy cupped my elbow and drew me forward. I swallowed, chucked it in, and watched it explode into a spurt of flame. I forgot to cross myself, watching hard to make sure it disappeared forever. Once I couldn't tell my slip from the ashes I closed my eyes. Someone grabbed my hand. I jerked up, and saw it was Miguel.

They'd made a circle, and the girl beside me took my other hand. Lucy started the prayer. "Dear Heavenly Father, we are Yours. Help us to remember Your promise, and help us to trust in You."

Such a short prayer, packed with all kinds of meaning. For one thing, what kind of promises had He made to me? Why would I trust Him? Why would He expect someone like me to trust Him, anyway? He probably knew better.

Lucy started another song, not a religious one, but one I'd heard on the oldies station. "Wind Beneath My Wings."

I'd always liked that song, always liked pretending that maybe someday somebody would hold me up, help me out. Lately in my dreams it had been Jackson, or, if not Jackson, someone who looked and talked just like him, only not as popular. I looked across at Shannon and gave up on that idea. Besides, he might be nice enough to drag me to the meeting. He was nice to everyone, but that didn't mean he cared.

The song ended and everyone trailed back inside. Miguel gave my hand a tug. I shook my head. "Aw, come on, Aidyn," he said, but I ignored him, and he finally left me to join his friends. I'd wait until I was alone and make sure the lump that held all my fears had really been destroyed.

"What did you think of your first meeting?"

I hadn't heard Lucy come back outside. I stared up at her. Tall, hair as dark and curly as mine, but she pulled it away from her face so she looked like a model. I pushed my glasses onto my nose, to remind myself they were there. "Um, yeah." I realized I hadn't answered her question. "I mean, I thought it was—"

"You put in a prayer."

I hoped she wouldn't ask what it had been.

She didn't. "I'm glad." She smiled, but as her gaze followed the traffic speeding past, her smile faded. "Some people, they feel funny about joining in right away. Especially something like this. I was afraid you'd be put off, me talking about how people don't have enough faith." She looked back at me, biting her lip. "But we all can use more, you know?"

I glanced through the doors at the rest of the kids. No one seemed to notice Lucy out here with the intruder and the smoke.

"You OK?" she asked.

"Sure." I hesitated before I blurted, "I thought it was a joke."

"What? Our prayer service? We don't always burn them, you know."

"No, not because of that. Some guys were messing around, talking about dates and stuff."

She smiled again and I returned it, glad I hadn't

made her mad. "Maybe that's what's important to them. Or maybe they said that, and wrote something different. You never know what's going on in someone else's head." She tipped hers to study me. "And we've all got problems."

"No kidding."

She reached for me and I realized she heard my bitter pain. I hate giving anything away. "I gotta go. My mom—"

I bolted inside and saw Mom leaning against the door. I shook. I couldn't tell if she'd been drinking until I saw her walk or heard her talk, but I had no faith that she'd be OK. I had to get her away or they'd never want me back. I forced myself to stumble between a group of kids eating cookies and laughing.

"You leaving already?" Jackson's words spun me around.

I hadn't even noticed him. Ten minutes ago I'd have had my internal radar telling me his position, and now I'd given that up, too.

I shrugged, hoping he wouldn't look around and see Mom. "I gotta go."

He did, anyway. "Tell her hi from me." He caught her glance and waved.

She started toward us. I met her halfway and dragged her back out again. The smell engulfed me. Not booze but a perfume so strong she must have poured it on. Or had she taken to drinking it? Some people, desperate drunks, did that.

"I don't mind waiting." She stopped, looking like she expected me to bounce over to some group and join in like I belonged. "You aren't finished, are you?"

"It's OK, Mom." I held my breath on the smell and dragged her out the door. We passed under the doorframe, and I looked over my shoulder. The leftover haze of the fire drifted across Lucy, who watched me. I thought of the word I'd scrawled on my paper, fast and sloppy so no one could read it. It had burned up, I'd seen the ashes, I swear I had, but I was so afraid Mom would read it, read the word *Mom* written in my handwriting and wonder why.

I shook my head. "No. I don't want to stay."

4

Given a choice, I would not have spent the rest of that day with my mother. She didn't give me any choice, and I didn't have my usual escapes handy. No school. No babysitting jobs. I couldn't even pretend I had a lot of cleaning to do around the apartment. She'd done it all the day before—*my* fault.

She'd also gone through my closet. How she had the gall to do that I don't know. It's *my* stuff in there, and when she told me, it was as if she thought I'd have no reason to be upset. She said, "Your shoes are in pretty bad shape. Most of them have holes in them."

I gaped at her and finally asked, "What were you doing looking at my shoes?"

She didn't tell me. "Why don't we go get you a new pair?" She smiled, like it was some sort of brilliant idea. I suppose, for someone who'd spent the last five years ignoring everything that had to do with her daughter, it was a big step. "Where do you like to buy shoes?"

That was rich. "The thrift store, Mom," I said. "That's the only place you can get them with holes already in them." Even though the Donaldsons overpay me every time I sit for them, it doesn't stretch far.

She blinked at me, all confused. "Don't you like new shoes?"

I rolled my eyes. "How should I know? When was

the last time you bought me new ones?" For my dad's funeral, probably.

I guess she remembered that, too. Her face went pale, but she just nodded. "All right, I give up. I'm buying you some shoes, that's all." As if she had to force me.

So I ended up with a pair of sneakers that no one else had worn before. They felt tight in all kinds of odd places, and every time I looked down, one of the laces had come undone. I felt like a first-grader, re-tying my shoes and doing a terrible job on it.

I thought of asking her why. We could afford a better apartment or take a cruise with all the money she'd save, now it wasn't all going for booze. But just because it had been almost a week since she'd taken a drink didn't mean she'd never start again.

"There," she said as we got back to the car. "That's taken care of."

As if all the years I had to hustle babysitting jobs just so I could buy someone else's crap from the thrift store had been erased by one tiny show of being a good mommy.

"This'll cut into your booze money."

"Aidyn!" Mom's face went white and her shoulders heaved. "I know—heaven knows I neglected you. I cheated you out of so much—"

"So what do I have to pay this time?"

Her hand holding the keys up to the ignition shook. "I'm not asking you to pay anything. I'm the one who gave up drinking."

"So you're thinking you'll save what, a couple of hundred a week? More than that?" But she only bought the cheap stuff.

Mom yanked on the gearshift like it was my neck,

and put it into drive. "I am trying so hard. And I've said I'm sorry. Can't you try? Maybe try to forgive me, just a little?"

"Is that what this is for? A bribe? If I'm nice, will you buy me something else?"

She glared at me and nodded. "OK, you want to call it that, fine. I'll make a deal with you. This pair of shoes for a week of good behavior, how's that?" Without looking at me again, she pulled out of the parking lot.

"No, thanks." I spun the box toward her and it clipped her jaw. "I never have learned how to be nice."

Her hands tightened on the wheel. "Never mind, Aidyn. I just keep hoping, that's all." She pushed the empty box back at me and drove to the grocery store.

Shopping went fast since I refused to talk. A few times Mom asked me if I wanted something particular. I'd shrug. I would not give her another weapon against me. I trailed after her and pretended she bought decent food every day. After she loaded the last gallon of milk into the cart and said, "Let's go," she headed up the one aisle we hadn't gone through, and turned back so fast she nearly plowed me down.

The booze aisle. No wonder. I caught up to her and grabbed the side of the cart. "What's the matter? Afraid of meeting your demon lover?"

When I saw her expression I felt like the devil myself, screaming insults I didn't understand because of my own hurt feelings.

"Are you ever going to stop?" Her question broke; she swallowed and pulled away. I couldn't answer, and she said, "Do you want me to start drinking again?"

"No," I whispered.

"I'll never forget that I'm a drunk. Even if you never say another word about it. I promise I will never forget."

I wouldn't either. But I'd hurt her, and I hated feeling so ashamed.

After we put the food away and our cupboards looked happier, Mom dragged me out for a walk. Anyone would have thought that we'd never argued. Mom had always been like that, I suppose, able to shrug off disagreements, but I never realized it was something that would stay after the drunk wore off.

"Aren't you mad at me?" I asked.

Her mouth tightened. "I'm trying as hard as I can to make this work." She shoved her keys in her pocket and tied a sweater around her waist.

"Mom." She looked at me, not angry, not impatient, just waiting until I whispered, "I'm sorry."

Her smile came quick and surprised. "That's all right, baby."

As soon as we reached the courtyard between the long arms of our apartment building I had to tie my shoe again. Mom waited, idly studying what used to be a rose garden. As I straightened, she shook her head. "What a waste. This could be a beautiful place, but the landlady never lets anybody do anything about it."

I wasn't interested in gardens. "How come you won't yell at me unless you're drunk?"

She shoulders sagged, and she turned away, shaking her head.

"I mean it. It's like you have to drink up enough courage to tell me what a rotten, selfish kid I am. And when you sober up—"

"I feel so guilty I want to die," she whispered. She

hurried across the street without looking. I let her get as far as the corner before I caught up.

She waited for the light to change, her arms crossed, hugging herself. "What I say when I'm drunk is not the truth."

I snorted and marched toward the thrift store across the street. My reflection glared at me from the dusty windows. I looked angry, but I could never explain. Not to Mom, not to anyone.

My shoelace had come loose again and I stopped. "What about all the times you said you hate me? What about that?"

Mom grabbed my arm and jerked me upright. "Aidyn, that's not the truth."

"I don't believe you."

Both her mouth and the fingers gripping my arm went slack and she backed away. Something slammed into my thighs. Lucas shouted, "Aidyn!"

Mrs. Donaldson, coming out of the thrift store behind him, tried to smile. It wavered and slid away when I glared at her.

"He saw you and had to come say hi," she said. By then Lucas had climbed halfway up my leg, so I shifted him to my hip and looked at Mom.

She ignored me, just looked at Mrs. Donaldson, who blushed, shrugged and finally said, "How you doing, Beth?"

Mom nodded. "All right. You?"

As Mrs. Donaldson explained why she'd left Andy home with her husband, Lucas grabbed my face, turning my head so we were eye to eye.

"Where are you going?"

I shrugged. "For a walk."

"Can we go with you?"

I set him on the sidewalk. "If your mom doesn't mind."

"Mommy, Aidyn says we can walk with them, 'K?"

Mrs. Donaldson tried another sick smile and glanced at Mom, who held her hand out as if to say, please come.

Lucas grabbed my hand and pulled. "We heard you from inside."

"Yeah. Your mom said you saw me."

He stopped to frown up at me. "Didn't. I *heard* you. We were looking at shirts, and I heard you yelling at your mommy." His hands went to his hips.

"Lucas," Mrs. Donaldson said.

"You weren't yelling *loud*," Lucas went on. "I just heard you a little."

Mom choked like she wanted to laugh. I spun away. Lucas called my name, and I heard Mom and Mrs. Donaldson laughing. My shoelace tripped me up, and I slammed the sidewalk, all my weight sliding me on my knees across the cement. Pain shot up my bones and into my stomach.

After a minute, I rolled to a crouch and poked at the new rip in my jeans. Lucas patted my shoulder, but I shrugged him off.

How could Mom laugh about me yelling at her? Or was she laughing at my embarrassment? If I'd realized everyone knew I was a drunk, I wouldn't be able to laugh at all. I'd want to die.

Lucas squatted next to me and stuck his head between my head and knee. "No blood," he announced. "You'll live."

By then Mom and Mrs. Donaldson had caught up.

"Are you OK?" Mom asked. Once again, she

pulled me up. "I'm not sure those shoes were such a good idea."

"I just need different laces or something," I muttered.

Lucas took my other hand. "We'll help you cross the street. Better be careful, Aidyn." He turned to study the colors of the stop light.

I glanced over my shoulder and caught Mrs. Donaldson giving me one of her "poor kid" looks, and Mom, giving Mrs. Donaldson a look even stranger.

"I quit drinking," Mom said.

"I noticed."

Mom snorted. She turned to Mrs. Donaldson, snorted again and in seconds they were both hysterical. I glared at them. What was so funny?

I wanted to cry. Die. Disappear. Like I already had.

After a minute Mom tried to calm down. "Margie, you are the best." She grabbed Mrs. Donaldson's arm as if they were friends, as if Mrs. Donaldson wasn't the pity queen for Mom's poor, neglected little kid, and started to laugh again. The two of them staggered across the street, howling, and my heart sank. So that was it. Mom had lied. Well, not exactly lied. She *had* stopped drinking but she must have started up again.

Lucas dragged me after our mothers. If I hadn't been so scared he'd steer me into a car, I'd have shut my eyes. Mom thought she could fool Mrs. Donaldson, and I guess she could, but not me. She couldn't fool me. She'd started drinking again, and it must feel so good to her to think how Mrs. Donaldson, at least, believed her lies.

5

On Monday I rushed to my usual lunch break hiding place as soon as I finished eating. Jackson managed to catch me just as I dragged open the heavy library door.

"Lucy's mailing you a map." He held onto the door and kept me from shutting it on him.

"To where?" I figured he'd tell me some stupid joke, like, to China.

"To her house. She handed them out at the meeting, but you'd gone by then."

I couldn't think of anything more intelligent than, "Oh?" so I said nothing. I leaned on the door's edge, balancing my weight with it. In a minute, Mrs. Swenson would yell at me to shut it, and I'd have an excuse to leave Jackson outside, with me safe in the library's silence.

"We're having a pizza party Friday night. You have to come."

"I have to?" I bounced the door on my hip to get Mrs. Swenson's attention.

He grinned. "We all decided. Naw, just kidding. But everyone's invited, and Lucy wanted me to make sure you knew about it. I'll pick you up if you don't have a ride. I'm getting Shannon, too." He leaned on the door, smiling.

Inside I cringed. Ever since I'd started high school, I'd longed for him to notice me. Now he had, and it was not what I'd imagined it would be. Not at all.

"Where is Shannon, anyway?"

He shrugged. "She didn't come to school today. Why?"

"I just figured she'd be with you." And where was Mrs. Swenson?

"Yeah? So don't forget the party, OK?"

I said, "OK," only because he seemed to be waiting for an answer.

"Great. Let me know if you need a ride." He took off, just in time for Mrs. Swenson to notice I'd been air conditioning the whole campus and yell at me.

****

When the phone rang that night I never thought it would be for me until Mom said, "No, this is Beth." I hate when people think she's me. Do I sound like a falling-down drunk? But we both sounded sober now.

She handed me the receiver. I didn't understand her smirk until I heard Jackson's voice.

I turned my back on her, though I couldn't stop her from listening. "How'd you get my number?"

"Phone book? I just called to find out if your mom is bringing you Friday or if you need me."

Did I need him? I closed my eyes. I hadn't daydreamed about him since the youth group meeting. I'd been too scared it would betray me somehow, show on my face or in my voice or write itself across the sky.

"I don't know."

"So ask her."

"OK." I waited for him to say good-bye or hang up, but he didn't. "I'll let you know tomorrow." But only if he asked and for that he would have to track me to earth and drag my *no* out of me.

"Ask her now. She's right there."

So I had to explain about the pizza party. Mom looked so delighted, and I couldn't figure out how to tell her I didn't want to go without starting an argument.

"That's wonderful," she said. "As long as I know where you are and who you're with."

I sighed. "Mom'll take me, I guess." Neither one seemed to notice my lack of enthusiasm. Why was I so careful not to hurt their feelings? Or was I just worried about mine?

The week we spent waiting for the party grated like rough gravel on both Mom and me. She wandered our small apartment, restless and jerky. She twitched leaves off her precious plants until I thought she'd kill them all. She scraped her nails through her hair and tugged at her clothes as if they bound her too tightly. I thought she might be less likely to go off on a binge if I stuck close by, but she got on my nerves. The only reason she left the apartment, besides work, was for her meetings. And she'd reek of that sickening perfume when she got home.

I never caught her at it, but I was sure she'd started drinking again, at least a little. Why else would she pour on perfume? But she managed to stay sober enough to fool everyone else.

Thursday night I got home from another babysitting job and found her squatting on the floor, surrounded by half-filled photo albums and stray pictures of Dad.

I saw one under the edge of the couch, and I fished it out, glancing at it before I gave it to her. Mom had taken it on our last camping trip. Daddy had been so sick by then. His bones cut through his skin as his brittle arms held me, his smile too wide in his gaunt face. I didn't remember that trip that way, though. I sagged against the couch and closed my eyes, and the scent of wood smoke hugged me, just the way it always clung to Dad's clothes. I felt the pebbles slipping under my feet as we walked to the beach. I remembered toasting marshmallows he couldn't eat, and making faces in the light of the ones that caught fire. I remembered the three of us wrapped together in sleeping bags as the flames died, and how we stayed that way all night, no one wanting to let go of the others even long enough to crawl inside the tent.

Mom held another picture from the same trip and her fingers curled around it, crumpling it.

"What are you doing? Don't ruin them." I snatched the picture and tried to flatten it.

"Sometimes I am still so mad at him," she whispered. "Why did he have to leave us? Don't you ever wonder?"

"He had cancer." Mom knew this. I backed away. She hadn't acted this confused in weeks. "It wasn't Daddy's fault."

"No, it's all mine. That's what you're saying, isn't it?" She looked up and I saw her tears. "Why am I the only one you hate? He's the one who left you."

I stood up, my heart pounding. "Mom?"

She dragged her hands though her hair, grabbing, pulling. "Sometimes I think I'm going crazy. I don't think I can do this." She thrust armfuls of photos back into the box. I knelt to help but she pushed my hands away, and I could only watch.

Did she want me to tell her I didn't hate her? If I did, would that be a lie? I tried to feel, really *feel*, how I felt about Mom, and all I knew was that I wanted to cry.

"Why'd you wreck his picture?"

She shrugged. "I just got angry. I don't think I meant to." She peered up at me, blinking.

"You're drunk."

"No." She stood and lifted the box in one easy movement, glaring at me as if to say, "See, I can still function. That proves it." Instead, she said, "You don't have to be drunk to ruin something."

She carried the box back to her room, and I stared after her. I'd *expected* her to be sober. Depended on it. Now, I wondered, and wondering hurt so much. Hadn't I learned? I couldn't depend on her.

Mom came back into the living room before I could escape with my pain, holding out the picture I'd picked up. "You keep this. You remember him, don't you, baby? You remember how much he loved us?"

I nodded, swallowed. As I took the picture, I wiped away a drop and wondered, whose tear?

"He wanted us to learn to be happy again. He wanted so much for us." Mom pulled the curtain away from the window. "Happiness, health, strength. All the things he had to give up."

"Daddy was happy." I stroked his printed face. Wouldn't he want me to be happy, too, and safe? Heart-safe, in a place where I didn't hope, didn't take any risks by depending on Mom. Daddy believed in risks. He climbed mountains. He camped in the wild. He trusted people who could hurt him. He'd trusted Mom and me. He didn't think much of safety. Yet I craved it.

By Friday, I was so ready for that party. I didn't want to be around the kids from the youth group, but I needed an escape from Mom. Her edgy mood had grown explosive. At times I wanted her to give in, get the waiting over with. But for once, I knew better than to tell her.

She came home late that evening and tossed an armful of library books onto the coffee table. I straightened them into a neater pile and she glared.

"When's this party of yours?" she growled.

"In forty-five minutes."

"You getting dinner there?"

"They said it's a pizza party. Last I heard that meant they'd feed us."

"Don't start with me, Aidyn."

I stomped into the bathroom and smeared mascara under my lashes and inside my glasses, but I heard Mom mumbling in the hall. I had to scrape the lenses with my nails to get the black off. Why did I bother? No one would see my eyes anyway.

"What time is this thing over?" Mom called through the door.

"Jackson said he'd bring me home by ten."

"Jackson said?" Her voice rose. "I thought I was coming back to get you. Is this a date?"

"With you driving me? Hardly. He just offered to bring me home."

"Oh, so I'm only allowed to drive one way?"

"Mom—" I yanked the door open to argue, but she interrupted.

"I'll pick you up. I don't want some crazy kid bringing you home."

That would have been funny if it hadn't been so scary. "You just don't want me to go." Well, I didn't either. Better to pick a fight now than to get there and be miserable and alone. Then, as the silence stretched, I realized I was right. "I might as well stay home. That's what you want, and you always end up getting your way."

She sucked in a long breath and stared at me though slitted eyelids. I knew what she wanted. She wanted me to stay home so she'd have someone stronger than she was to keep her from drinking. How could she think I could do that? I never had before. I wasn't strong.

"Fine!" I slammed out of the bathroom door, as mad that I'd wasted mascara as anything else. "I'll stay home. Jackson'll figure out I'm not coming."

"I never said you couldn't go."

"No, that's just what you want, though, isn't it?"

She bit her lip and looked away.

I jerked my sweater over my head and threw it on my bedroom floor. "So I'll stay home and hold your hand or whatever I'm supposed to do—"

"I don't need you to babysit me!"

"Don't you?"

She rubbed her eyes and seemed to shrink. "Yeah." The word came out in a sigh. "You're right, baby. I feel like I could use a little support tonight, but I'm not going to get it from you, am I?" She followed me and picked up my sweater, holding it out to me. "But I'm picking you up."

"No—"

"Aidyn, I'll pick you up."

All I could see were horrible pictures in my mind. After hours of getting wasted, Mom would come careening down night streets looking for me. If she remembered she had promised she'd get me. If she hadn't passed out. "I want Jackson to bring me home."

Her lips pinched together. "Does he know you

have a crush on him?"

"I don't. I just don't want to die tonight."

She screamed. The sound filled my head, guttural, frustrated, like sand. I covered my ears and crouched to hide and knew I couldn't go anywhere.

When I uncurled she'd gone.

I heard her car peeling from the carport. Even if I'd wanted to go, I couldn't. I had to wait for Mom to get home, to clean her up. Or wait for a call from the police.

And it would be my fault. Whatever happened to Mom now would be my fault.

I'd had a week to forget that shame and fear, and it had stolen the time to grow bigger than I could handle. I couldn't stuff it back inside. It exploded out of my mouth and scared me as much as Mom's scream had. Besides, how could I hide from myself?

I bolted outside, charged down the stairs and stopped on the curb. What did I think I could do? Find her? I could only wait for her to stagger home with her booze, get whatever she had left over away from her, and wait until she got sober enough to listen when I begged her to stop.

I hadn't done that in a long time.

A car skidded in front of me, and Mom reached across to open the passenger door. "Is he coming to get you?"

Relief filled my heart and to hold it in, I wrapped my arms around my waist. "No."

"Are you ready to go then?" She acted as though nothing had happened. "Come on, I'll take you. Where's the map that girl sent you?"

I pulled it from my pocket, and Mom studied it before she took off again. "Did you call him?"

"Jackson? No. Why?"

"Why were you waiting outside?"

"I don't know." I shrugged. "Maybe looking for you." But the "maybe" made it a lie.

"Why?"

"Maybe I don't want you making love to a bottle, OK?"

She drove for a long time, her knuckles white on the steering wheel, her lip caught tight between her teeth. We stopped in front of a small house, and I checked the address. Lucy's, but I didn't want to get out. I didn't want to leave my mother like this and wondered what kind of sickness I had, to want the crap she put me through. But I didn't—I didn't.

I reached for the door handle, and she slid her hand toward me, as if she needed to anchor me. "Honesty's a good thing, isn't it? Thank you, baby." After a minute she released my hand. "I don't want that, either."

I turned my hand palm up and let hers rest in mine. I couldn't remember the last time I'd touched her willingly, except to clean her up or drag her someplace safer than where she'd passed out.

"Were you, Mom?" I whispered. "Is that where you were going?"

She closed her eyes. "Yes."

I tightened my fingers. "I don't want to go. I want to go home."

Mom laughed, though her tears almost made it a sob. "You're here, already. You're staying. I've wasted enough of your fun, haven't I?" In the shadows and streetlight tricks I saw more tears. "As much as I want you with me right now, I'm not going to keep you, OK?" She pulled my hand to her face, and I let my fingers curl against her cheek, slide on the loose, damp skin. "I know almost everything I've done has hurt you, baby, and I'm sorry."

"I won't have any fun."

"Yes, you will."

"I don't want to stay, Mom."

"Aidyn, I'm OK. I don't want a drink now. I want my daughter to go to this party and have fun with her friends."

"They're not—"

"They are. Go on. I'll call my sponsor when I get home, OK? Don't start worrying about me."

As if I'd ever stopped. "But Mom—"

"There's Jackson. Go on, Aidyn. I'm OK." She kissed my palm before I could pull away. Maybe I didn't want to. "Ten, right? I'll be here."

My door opened and Jackson leaned down. "Hey, Mrs. Pierce. Aidyn, you made it. Great. Come on."

I got out and tried to wait at the curb until Mom turned the corner, but Jackson hauled me up the walk and I didn't hear her engine start until he shut the front door behind me.

6

Inside the dim room, a rug covered the wood floors between the couch and some chairs. Miguel slumped on the couch, alone, a soda balanced on his stomach.

"You remember Miguel?" Jackson asked.

I nodded. "Who could forget him?" But the Miguel at Lucy's house seemed a different person from the clown I knew from school and church.

Jackson laughed, but his mirth died quickly. "We've got a tiny bit of a crisis in the other room. Shannon had a big fight with her mom, and now she's doing the meltdown. Would you mind letting people in for us?"

Without waiting to hear if either of us agreed, Jackson left. Poor little Shannon, I thought. Poor, lucky little Shannon. She has a fight with her mother, and the whole world shores her up. I have a fight with mine, and no one knows. I wondered what Shannon would do if she had to deal with my mom.

I wandered around the room, watched Miguel's soda rise and dip with his breathing. I edged to one of the chairs and perched on the seat. "Are you all right?" I whispered.

He shrugged. "My dad's hitting the bottle again." His voice came out flat, like he's been working hard at feeling nothing, and succeeded. "Had to get out before he started hitting me." He laughed and took a drink of soda while I froze, shocked.

Why was he telling *me*? Because he didn't know me? Maybe Jackson, the take-care-of-the-world-guy, should have stayed. Everybody turned to Jackson. Everybody but me. I wondered what Miguel would do when he realized he'd been talking to me, or if he'd learned not to care.

"This is the first party you've ever come to, isn't it?" Miguel asked. "I mean, with the group."

So he knew who I was, after all. "Yeah."

"You'll like it. Really." He laughed again, as though I ought to understand the joke. "Usually we're a lot more fun than this."

He stood and walked around, stretching his back and finishing off his soda. "I hate my dad. What's the point of quitting when you know you're just gonna start again? He never means it. Makes all kinds of promises, but he never means to keep them."

He paced, and I couldn't find an answer. He didn't seem to need one.

"Sometimes I think he does that so he can knock me and Mom down, you know? 'Cause we start to hope, and we think everything's gonna be normal. And then, nothing ever stays good, not around my house."

Or mine. Panic picked up my heartbeat's tempo. "It's stupid," I said. "Hoping is stupid. It never does any good. Just wastes time." Until everything crashed.

He grunted, and he looked as if he saw me for the first time—saw *me* and not my shadow. I wished I'd never said a word then took the wish back.

Miguel held out his empty can. "You want another one?"

I said, "Sure," even though I hadn't had a first one. When he brought it back, cold and moist and something to keep my hands busy, he sat down, leaning close. "Your dad?"

"What?"

"Your dad's a drunk?"

"He's dead."

"Oh. Sorry." He stared at his can, wiped a ring out of the frost. "I saw your mom Sunday, and she looked OK."

"She is."

He laughed softly and in the back of his throat. He didn't believe me, and I could tell I'd hurt him. He'd been open with me, after all. But how could I say anything more? And yet, before I could stop them, words poured out, words that I'd always heard in the silence of my head, when I cried to my Dad. I'd never even said them to the imaginary Jackson who cared.

"For right now, she's OK. I guess. She says she is, anyway."

And he nodded. "How long?"

I swallowed. "A week and a half. I think."

"Is that long for her?"

I nodded. Please, no more questions, no more words, no more hurts, no more.

"Is she in a program?"

"A program? You mean like AA?"

He nodded.

"She says she is."

"Yeah. That's good, you know? They work the program, and it's like they made a commitment. You're lucky. It might stick. Not my dad, though. He won't do no program." He took a long drink. "My mom, she does it, works it like crazy all the time, especially when he starts. But him? Nah. He's better'n all that."

I forgot Mom for a minute. "*Both* your parents?"

"Yeah, but Mom's been good for three years. Since my brother died. Guess how he died? Killed himself driving a motorcycle drunk. Idiot. And Dad's like, he doesn't even care. Me, I'm the one's never gonna touch that stuff. Look what it did to them."

As he talked, his voice grew rough, and I could tell he felt it. He wasn't just making words. I wondered if I could ever talk about my mother the way he did his, say my mom has been sober three years, and be proud. I wondered if I could talk about these last two weeks with the same kind of pride, or if I should.

"I don't want to do that either. Be a drunk. They're disgusting."

He snorted as the bell rang. I looked at him, but he seemed to have forgotten we were supposed to answer the door, so I let in what seemed like a dozen people, all armed with pizza boxes.

"Pizza's here!" Wallis pushed past me. "Hey, it's the quiet one. Where's Lucy? Where's the plates? I'm starving. Gonna eat the box too if she doesn't save it from me."

Lucy ran in, laughing, and in a minute they were all in the middle of a pizza party that headed to the kitchen. Miguel left, too, but I cowered in the dark room. I thought about sneaking outside, sitting on the porch until Mom showed up, but I couldn't work up the energy to move.

"Three years," I whispered to my hands. Dad had died almost seven years ago, when I was nine. And Mom had been drinking hard since then. I tried to look ahead three years. I'd be in college. Maybe. Maybe I'd be out on my own. I could see myself but not Mom. I put the can down carefully on a coaster and stood. I'd walk those few miles home.

"Aidyn?" Lucy tiptoed into her own living room. "What's wrong? Come and eat, girl."

"I'm not very hungry."

"Then come in and just hang out with us, OK? That's why we invited you."

We? Who was we? The whole group? Couldn't be. Shannon was part of it.

Lucy pushed me ahead of her into the lighted kitchen, and the first thing I saw was Miguel, wearing his clown-persona again, on his knees in front of Shannon, begging for something everyone else found hilarious but I hadn't heard.

I leaned against the oven and let Jackson hand me a slice dripping with cheese and extra grease, the paper plate nearly transparent under it. I didn't belong here, I never would. I had a secret, even if I couldn't keep it. And maybe that secret wasn't all about my mom.

After a while, people began moving around, and I threw what was left of my pizza in the trash. I followed a couple of kids I didn't know into the backyard, and skirted a pool that reflected shine but no light.

I shouldn't have come. How could I be so stupid? I'd left Mom, and now she was probably bombed. I'd let Miguel know I didn't care enough to get excited that she'd managed a week and a half. And I'd ruined that all by myself. Not that it mattered. Nothing good ever lasted. I just reduced it to crap.

No wonder Miguel gravitated to Shannon. Who wouldn't? Normal Shannon lived a real life. Who would want to hang around someone who couldn't even laugh?

And me. Miguel's smile did more to my heart than jogging a straight mile. I couldn't catch my breath. Didn't want to. Out of nowhere, I fell for a pair of brown eyes when I'd been dying to catch the attention of blue. Fickle me. Did normal girls fall in and out of love and back in again, in an instant? But I'd abandoned lusting after Shannon's boyfriend and latched onto the boy who lusted after her. Human, I might be. Sane, never. I hated being Shannon's shadow.

More people must have come because they spilled into the yard and noise rose to match the pound of music inside. I ducked around a corner and found a tiny space where a cinderblock wall met a wooden gate. Hunched down, I stared at the light shimmering from the water. I wasn't hiding, just waiting the party out. Just waiting to find out what kind of shape Mom had gotten herself into.

I'd call and ask her to come early. I should have done it a long time ago. Mom would have been a lot safer if I had. But I didn't know where Lucy's phone was, and I didn't want to go looking for her and then have to interrupt her. I didn't want to make everyone wonder what I wanted, wonder why I didn't have my own cell phone, wonder why I had to call my mom in the middle of such a great party.

I'm sick. I need to go home.

I stood up and heard Miguel's voice, singing to one of the old songs Lucy played. "Have you seen her? Tell me, have you seen her?"

He danced across the concrete strip around the pool, and I slipped behind him and pretended I'd just come out of the house. No way would I let him catch me crouching in a corner like the kid everyone forgot during hide-and-seek.

"Yup, I've seen her," he said as he turned. "Whatcha doing all by yourself?"

I shrugged.

"What scared you off? Did I scare you?"

"No. I'm not scared."

Miguel jerked his head toward a bench at the end of the pool. I followed and sat next to him, wondering all over again. Some feeling filled me, and though I couldn't name it, it pressed tears to my eyes.

Miguel sat with his elbows on his knees so he had to twist around to look at me. "You know, most people, they go to a party, they talk to the other people there. That's how most people do parties."

I had to laugh. "Yeah, but I don't know anyone."

"Oh, so I'm nobody."

"Nobody *else*, I mean."

"How you gonna know them if you won't talk to them?"

I shrugged again.

"You mad 'cause you told me about your mom?" Before I could argue, he leaned closer. "The first time is the hardest, you know? After that, you find out you don't die when you tell someone. You find out it's OK to talk about that stuff. It's not your fault."

What I'd told him wasn't my fault, no. But if Mom showed up sloshed, or didn't show up at all, *that* would be my fault. And that was something I would never tell anyone.

"Aidyn," he said. "It's OK for people to know."

"I figured everyone knew anyway. Shannon must have told everyone. She must have told Jackson, at least."

"And sometimes you think everyone's talking about you?"

Except for the times I knew they don't see me at all.

"Yeah, well, what does Shannon know, anyway?" He stared over the pool, his fingers twisting in complicated patterns. "It's OK to have fun."

"Yeah. Sure. I'm having fun."

He grinned. "I know what it's like. You get so scared, or so mad, and how can you have fun when anything could happen? But you have to. You'll go crazy if you don't."

"So that's my problem."

That time he laughed. "Not hardly. You're not crazy, Aidyn. Come on." He grabbed my hand and pulled me to my feet before I could jerk away, and he didn't let go until we got to the living room again, now dimly lit by candles and crowded with kids and the sound system's vibrations.

The smell of cold pizza roiled in my stomach. I wanted my corner back, but if I ran out I'd look like an idiot, so I sat on the floor next to Miguel and reminded myself to pretend I was having fun. If only I could figure out how.

Miguel handed me another soda, though I didn't want it. I'd already wasted enough of Lucy's stuff. I hunched over it and pretended I didn't mind that he didn't stay with me but meandered around the room talking to others. After a few minutes, though, more kids wandered inside, and he made his way back to where I sat. He stopped for a minute to jibe at Dan, describing something from basketball practice, and made Wallis laugh.

Shannon plopped on the couch across the room. I could see she'd been crying. Funny how, even after three years of not even talking to her, I still knew her so well. I saw the way her thumb tucked through her belt loop, and knew it meant she'd relaxed. She knew how to have a good time, even if she'd started out a mess.

Jackson, picking his way between legs stretched across the carpet, stopped to say something to her and Shannon grinned but didn't move. That surprised me.

"Aidyn, this is Stephanie." Miguel had to yell next to my ear so I could hear him. He pointed to the girl on my other side. She waved, and I waved back, and we settled into the privacy of too much noise.

The music pounded across the floor, up through my bones and out my fingertips. I couldn't hear voices, just saw faces mouthing, laughing, frowning, flirting. The room kaleidoscoped in my head, breaking something open, hurting. I decided I hated parties. I'd given it a try and now I could say I didn't party, if anybody ever asked me again.

I snorted. Who would ask me?

The music went dead and surprised voices called out.

"Circle time." Lucy carried a sheaf of papers to the middle of the room, nudged aside a few feet, and threatened to use somebody as a chair before we'd shifted enough to make room for her. Someone scooted me toward Miguel. I pulled my knees up and wrapped my arms around them.

"Hey, you know the rules," Miguel shouted. "You come to a party at Lucy's you gotta pay. I mean, pray."

Lucy made a face at him before she laughed with everyone else. People shoved closer, and I couldn't back up because of Miguel's shoulder behind me.

"We're supposed to pray," Lucy said, and began as simply as she had on Sunday, with the same request for centering. I wished I knew what that meant. I wished I had the guts to ask, but that'd show my stupidity. She'd know how very much I didn't belong if I let on how much I didn't know.

"God, You have blessed us so much, even in our need You have given Yourself to us." I squeezed my eyes shut and clenched my hands. Blessed? I *really* didn't belong here.

Lucy stopped. I waited for her "amen" but she left us in our silence. I studied the other kids, their faces solemn or blank, each of us alone with our own thoughts. I had no idea what I was supposed to be thinking or praying.

I almost choked when beside me Stephanie said, "God, thanks for the help on that cruddy test. I had to pass it, and You didn't let me down."

We had to pray out loud? That was worse than writing prayers on paper. I tried to roll to my knees, to bolt, but had no room. I swallowed my panic and tried to melt into the silence that followed her prayer. I would *not* pray out loud.

Wallis spoke up. "Those people who lost their homes in the flood, God, we pray You bless them. Provide what they need."

I am so stupid, I don't even know what flood he's talking about.

Another voice. "My dad might lose his job. His company's downsizing."

"My brother got caught shoplifting. He's fourteen."

"It seems like half the people at school are doing drugs lately. Please make them stop using. Please."

The prayers came from islands of faces in the darkness. I couldn't always tell who spoke, and hoped no one would notice that I hadn't.

Lucy's voice. "My little brother's thinking of

A Fistful of God

moving in with his girlfriend. Pray for guidance."

Another silence. "Praise report. I got accepted at the art school I wanted, *with* a scholarship." At that, more voices chimed in, thanking God.

"My dad's drinking again," Miguel said.

I turned to watch him, but he had his head down, hiding his eyes. "Mom said if he hits me again, even if he doesn't break anything this time, she'll call the cops."

"Good, we'll pray for your mom to be strong," someone said.

"Yeah. Thanks. I know it's coming. If I hadn't come tonight I'd've been pulp."

After another silence, and he added quietly, "If Mom doesn't call the cops, pray I live through it so I can."

I felt movement and glanced back. Stephanie had her arms around Miguel's shoulders, rocking. His head tipped back, now, his eyes closed, and he leaned into her the way I'd seen Lucas fold into his mother. The sight sent shivers over my arms.

"Praise report." This time it was Shannon. "I forgot to tell you guys because I was so mad at her, but now I have to say thanks, because I really do love my mom. Anyway, her cancer is in remission."

Shock ripped through my stomach, and I stared at her. How could someone like Shannon's mom get cancer? She wouldn't *let* it happen, would she?

"And then pray she can let me make some of my own decisions."

I turned and saw Miguel watching me. He reached out and covered my hand with his, exactly the same way Mom had in the car. I choked and looked up, ready to say a prayer, ask for their prayer, at least. God would listen to them, wouldn't He, even if He didn't want to hear from me?

"Anyone else?" Lucy asked the silence. My prayer slithered into my throat and cowered there. I closed my eyes and my mouth and hoped Miguel couldn't tell what I'd been about to do.

"OK, God, You've heard us. Please hear, as well, those prayers unsaid, those too secret to be told. Amen."

I wanted so badly for my prayer to be one of the ones He heard, anyway.

People began to move, though Miguel stayed next to Stephanie. I sneaked outside and wandered to the far side of the pool in case Miguel came out to check my corner. He didn't. I squatted on the edge to push at the leaves floating on the surface and took a deep breath.

God, please, help Mom. Don't let her get drunk tonight. Ever, OK? Make her not want to anymore. Make her not be an alcoholic, please? Oh, I'd gotten to be so daring, hadn't I, using that *word* even though no one heard, no one but God. I hoped. *Please.*

I'd thought praying was meant to make a person peaceful, but I felt worse. Panic burned through me. If I'd wanted Mom to stay sober, I should have stayed with her and *made* her. I ran into the house. I had to find some way to get home.

The empty kitchen smelled like sweet soda and pizza boxes. Lucy walked in as I froze, fighting the panic. "Oh, Aidyn, I told Miguel you must have gone home. He was looking for you, but he left. I'm sorry."

"That's OK. I need to go home, too, but I need—I don't have a cell phone—"

"Sure, here." She handed me a cordless from its

base on the counter. "Next time you don't need to ask."

Jackson came in with a grocery bag stuffed with squashed cans. "Shannon's waiting. You ready?"

"My mom said she was coming."

"What time?'

"Ten. I told her ten." I wrapped my arms around me and shook.

Lucy looked at the clock. "She's late. I bet she fell asleep." She grinned. "My mom always used to do that. It drove me crazy."

Falling asleep was so different from passing out.

I dialed but our line was busy. I shook so badly I couldn't get the phone into the cradle. Past ten, Mom would *not* have called her sponsor so late. Joyce, sure. Joyce stayed up all hours, drinking. Encouraging Mom to take another drink.

God, why couldn't You have answered even one of my prayers?

I looked around and saw Shannon hanging onto Jackson's arm, frowning. She knew.

"I'll call my mom." I jerked to stare at Jackson while he dialed. "Mom, I need to give Aidyn a ride home after all. Her mom didn't make it, and she's kind of upset—"

How did he know?

"OK, OK," he finished. He turned to me. "She said to wait another fifteen minutes, and if your mom's not here, to go ahead and take you."

"Fine. Whatever." He was doing me a favor, I wouldn't argue. I thanked Lucy and stumbled to the sidewalk. I should have stayed home. I should have.

A tree blocked the streetlamp, and I leaned against its trunk, pressing so the bark dug into my skin. How could she do this to me? I bet Shannon was busy telling them why Mom was late. Why she wouldn't show.

Lucy's front door slammed, and I heard Shannon. "Even if she shows up, we'd probably better not let her go—you know. She's probably—"

"Shannon—" Jackson started.

"You've never seen her. I have. It's scary—she gets so drunk."

Jackson tried to interrupt again but Shannon talked over him.

"It scares Aidyn, and she's too tough to get scared easy."

Tough. Right, only, not me. I'm not tough.

Jackson raised his voice. "It'll be OK, I promise."

How could he promise anything?

Shannon started up again and Jackson said, "Not so loud."

"She's not out here."

I pushed away from the tree and stumbled up the walk, staggering just like my mother, only my unsteadiness came from anger. "We might as well go. She's not coming."

Shannon squealed and slapped her hand over her mouth. Jackson shook his head. "Wait one more minute, OK?" he begged, just as a car pulled up to the curb.

Mom got out. "Sorry, Aidyn. I couldn't find that map, and I got turned around." She smiled and the fear soured my throat until I saw that her steps were steadier than mine had been. "Hi, Jackson," she went on.

"Hey, Mrs. Pierce. You made it." He moved off the porch, and Shannon came with him, holding onto his arm as if afraid he'd sprint away, or afraid my crazy, drunken mother would visit some unnamed evil on her. We stood in Lucy's front yard, waiting for Mom to act like she planned to get back in the car and take me home.

"Shannon?" Mom sounded delighted. "I haven't seen you in a long time." From the way she acted, I knew she had no idea why.

"I guess not," Shannon said, more embarrassed by the second. She looked down and let her hair curtain her face.

I ran to the car and yanked the door open.

"Tell your mother thanks again, Jackson," Mom said.

After she started the engine I said, "I didn't know you knew Jackson's mother."

She hesitated. "We met a few weeks ago."

"She called you, didn't she? Tonight, I mean, and told you to come get me."

Mom sighed. "Jackson said you were upset."

"I wasn't." I pushed myself against the door. "I figured you were too drunk to remember."

"I know." Mom pulled into our carport. "I wish I could help you, Aidyn, but I guess you want to do it for yourself. You won't let anyone else in."

Who would want in to help *me*?

7

I lay on my side in bed and stared at blinds broken by age. The dark night rendered them fuzzy. Chunks of streetlight wrestled their way through the holes.

I did not want to hang around the kids from church anymore. Any kids. They all had so much more than I did—fun, friends, families, people they could trust. I would never be like them. They knew it, and I knew it. No matter how hard I tried, I couldn't hide Mom, or hide what she was. I couldn't hide me, or my fear. And if I could, Shannon would blow my cover.

Tears trickled down my face, and I sniffled before I realized what I was doing. I sat up and grabbed a tissue to blow my nose. I was not going to cry just because I wanted to be like everyone else. I wanted it so bad, and I didn't know how to get it. But crying never helped.

Miguel knew. He was one of them, even though he was like me. How could he do that, be two different people?

I remembered how Lucy said Miguel had been looking for me. He knew all about me, but he'd still come looking for me. Because he recognized me? I closed my eyes and remembered his prayer and prayed it over in my mind, until it melted into my heart. Until I fell asleep.

****

A Fistful of God

The next morning the gardener's lawnmower coughing itself to death woke me, and after that, Mrs. Roth, our landlady, started yelling. She yelled at a lot of people, though it seemed she yelled the most at Mom. Either Mom was late with the rent, or she'd done something to tick off one of the other tenants.

The gardener argued back. I rolled over, deliciously knowing this one time, Mom wasn't the problem. But Mrs. Roth's heels rang on the stairs and then our bell sounded, and before I could crawl out of bed to let her in, Mom answered. I pulled the pillow over my head, but no matter how I stretched my legs and arched my toes, I couldn't shake the jumpy fear. I sneaked into the kitchen to listen.

"All right, then." Mrs. Roth shuffled a pile of papers on the table and sent some of them flying to the floor. I scrabbled them together and handed them over then rummaged in the fridge for some juice.

"Thank you—ah—dear," she said.

I looked over my shoulder. Mom didn't look at all worried, so I relaxed. Still, I figured I had to stand sentinel, to protect us from the wicked landlady who'd love to kick us out.

"Even so, Mrs. Pierce," Mrs. Roth said. "Even so, I want it done in the morning. Not too early. But in the morning. You understand?"

Mom caught my eye and grinned. So what was so important that Mom had to do it in the morning, probably because Mrs. Roth figured she wouldn't be bombed yet? Hadn't Mrs. Roth ever seen her with a hangover? Probably not, I decided. Mom liked to stay in bed for those, or just get drunk all over again. I saw nothing in that to share a joke over, though.

"What's your best time?" Mrs. Roth asked.

Mom shrugged. "Midnight? I don't suppose you want the weed eater going then, though, do you?"

Mrs. Roth dragged in a hard breath and held it. Mom smiled, and it wasn't a nice smile, either. "Sorry. Actually, early Saturday morning is good for me."

"Not too early." Mrs. Roth turned to me. "You'll remind her if she forgets, won't you?"

"Remind her about what?"

"The yard work," she said. "The garden. You won't let her forget unless it's—um—better if she forgets."

"You mean if she's drunk?" Why I asked, I don't know. I've never thought Mom's alcoholism funny. But Mrs. Roth looked like a lemon getting ready to lecture, and I didn't want to hear it. I wanted her to leave.

She ended up coughing and spitting all over the papers on our table. I thought Mom might choke from holding in her laughter.

"Child! Have you no respect?" Mrs. Roth stood and glared at Mom, wiping slobber off her chin as she stalked to our front door. "I suppose it's no wonder she's so disrespectful, but you'd think she'd not want to be like you."

For the first time in years, I was glad to know I was like Mom. After Mrs. Roth slammed the door Mom collapsed on the kitchen counter, laughing so hard I thought she'd fall. I watched her for a moment, decided she was laughing, just laughing and not bombed, before I turned back to the fridge. "You want some pancakes, Mom?"

"Sure." She gulped, choked again and finally straightened to wrap her arm around my shoulder. "You almost lost me a job, baby, but it would have been worth it."

I twisted to face her. "What happened to your job with Toni?"

"Nothing. This is extra. She's giving me a break on the rent, and we can use it."

"I thought…I thought we had more money now."

She held out her hands. "We're OK, but I had to take off a lot of days these last few weeks. Going through withdrawals doesn't make working easy. And it'll help to have something to do. I get…um…restless." She ruffled my hair. "I'll do whatever it takes to get through the day."

I shrugged, still not understanding but not expecting to. Mom handed me the beater, and I cracked an egg over the bowl. "I didn't…I mean…I never noticed you weren't at work or anything." I looked up. "I never noticed you were sick."

"That's all right."

I poured the first batch of pancakes, watched them bubble, watched them burn. Mom reached around me and flicked off the flame, dumped the ruined food in the trash and wiped the pan. "Aidyn, baby," she said. "Please—"

The phone rang.

"Don't," she started, but all I could think of was Miguel, and I grabbed it. "Let me talk to your mother," an unfamiliar voice said. I didn't know who this woman was, but I knew she didn't like me.

I handed over the phone and went back to cooking, and tried to pay attention to the food. Should I call Miguel? If he hadn't called me by tonight, I decided I would. I'd pretend I didn't know if the youth group met every week, and we'd start talking and then…

The second batch looked much better, and I took the plate into the living room for Mom. She had her back to me but still I heard her.

"I know Aidyn better than you do," she said, "and I think she can handle this."

I should have walked away, but I had the right to listen, didn't I?

"She's my daughter. My life. If it weren't for her I'd never have quit, and right now, anything can destroy our relationship. I don't want this to come between us." Silence, then, "She has to know. She'll find out soon enough, and how will I ever get her to trust me again? I think now…I think she's starting to."

I backed into the kitchen. *Did* I trust her? But if she'd kept something from me, something important, why should I? I'd never be able to eat now. I left everything on the table, made sure I'd turned off the stove, and crept to the shower. I came out to find Mom waiting.

"Aidyn, there's something I…" She bit her lip. "Please try to understand."

"Mom, what?"

She took a breath and wrapped her arms around herself. "I love you, baby. I don't want to ever hurt you."

I couldn't answer—I couldn't—but I leaned against her until she put her arms around me, and I let her hold me. For once, I let myself feel like I had my Mom back again, after missing both my parents for years and years.

****

Sunday morning I huddled at the end of the

church pew and watched the priest so I'd know the first second I could escape. I'd called Miguel, left a message with his mother, and he'd never called me back. I'd only gone to Mass at all because of that hug from Mom, and I was not waiting around to let those kids start on me again

"Come *on*, Mom." I grabbed her as soon as the service ended, but she resisted me, hanging back, looking across the parking lot crowd. I saw Shannon and figured Jackson couldn't be far behind. I turned and barreled into some lady.

Mom's horrible perfume-disguise engulfed me, just as a barely familiar voice said, "Beth!" Pieces clicked into place. She had called Mom the day before, the lady who didn't know me but didn't like me. She was why Mom smelled so horrible after she'd been out. The one who knew something she didn't want Mom to tell me.

"This is my daughter, Aidyn." Mom pushed me forward to meet the woman's ice-blue eyes. I'd seen those eyes before. I just couldn't think where. We glared at each other. "Aidyn, this is Elaine, my sponsor."

"So you're Aidyn." I figured she hoped I'd crawl back in my garbage-can home and never bother her again. "I've heard an awful lot about you."

Maybe it was the way she said "awful," maybe it was her eyes, but I shivered.

"She's as beautiful as you said, Beth." Once she'd gushed to Mom, she turned back to me. All the kindness she'd used talking to Mom disappeared. "How are you liking the youth group?"

"It's all right."

Jackson came up behind her, and I braced myself.

"Aidyn, you coming? We've got to get started."

I shrugged and watched Elaine turn to Jackson. "Come home as soon as the meeting ends. Dad wants an early start this afternoon."

"OK, yeah. I'll hurry." He grabbed my wrist. "Come on."

Who was he to be forever telling me to go somewhere?

As he dragged me toward the hall I looked back. Mom and Elaine stood close. Mom would reek later, and I wouldn't care. It was *not* a disguise, after all, not something to put me off the track of booze.

I stopped so fast that Jackson's hold on me nearly pulled my shoulder out of its socket. "Elaine is your mother."

"I know." He frowned. "You just now figured that out?"

"I've never met her before."

"Oh. I thought you had. Your mom spends a lot of time with her."

"She's Mom's sponsor. How'd she get to be a sponsor?"

He shrugged. "I don't know how they do those things in AA. I go to Alateen, but I think it's different."

I stared. *Jackson's* mother, too?

He tugged again, and I stumbled. As I righted myself I saw Shannon and Miguel in front of the hall, and I remembered my unreturned phone call. "Wait. Just a minute, OK? You knew about my mom and—and her—stuff." The Sunday before, when he'd first invited me to the youth group, flashed through my mind. "You even knew her before last week."

"I know." He wouldn't look at me.

I twisted my arm but his fingers tightened around

my wrist. I pulled my hand up so all the strength of my arm pushed against his thumb and broke his hold, and I bolted.

"Aidyn, come back here." I heard him behind me, but I didn't stop until I got to Mom's car. Though I knew she'd locked it, I jerked on the door handle, and when he reached for me I turned on him.

"You lied to me!"

"I didn't. I thought you knew—"

"How could I?" I pressed against the car as though I could melt into it.

"It wasn't up to me to tell you about it. I'm not even supposed to know the people Mom sponsors."

"But you do."

"I can't help it. Your Mom is over at our house a lot. She was there—" He looked away and back. I never thought I'd see Jackson embarrassed. "She was there right after she first quit, and she was so worried about you, you know? I said I knew you from school, and she asked me—" He hesitated. "Look, Aidyn, it wasn't like we set you up to hurt you. It was my mom's idea. She figured if you know what was going on you wouldn't have anything to do with me."

"She was right." But the truth was, she'd been wrong. *Now* I knew, and that was why I didn't want anything to do with him.

His fingers brushed my arm.

I jerked away.

"So you're gonna dump all your friends just because your mom was too scared to tell you she was worried about you?"

"What friends?"

"That's not fair." He hadn't yelled, but I could tell he was ticked. "What about Miguel? He's going through a really hard time, Aidyn. He needs friends."

I shrugged. Miguel didn't want me; I knew that much. "So go be his friend, why don't you?"

I stared at the black asphalt and didn't see his face, only his shoes in front of me.

"Maybe, just once, you could stop thinking about poor, poor Aidyn and think about someone else."

So now Jackson hated me as much as his mother did. I was so good at earning hatred.

"At least your mom's sober right now. You heard what Miguel said about his dad. He's been hanging out at my house since the party, but he has to go home sometime."

The shoes left.

I huddled against the side of Mom's car, shaking, and watched the last few kids hurry into the hall. I'd gotten my wish. I wasn't a part of that group anymore, if I ever had been.

But—Miguel. Jackson had been right about Miguel.

He sat in the last row with Jackson and Shannon, next to an empty seat. I wondered if he'd saved it for me. I slid in. Miguel turned to me, and his face lit up. I wondered if we'd get a chance to hold hands during another prayer. I wondered if Miguel would want to hold mine. I stared at my shoes and Miguel sat next to me. I missed the beginning of Lucy's talk, but it didn't matter, because through all her prayers and praise, my heart sang with hope.

8

I'd forgiven Miguel, though he'd done nothing; I'd come close to forgiving Jackson. I'd gone to his meeting, hadn't I? But not Mom. On the ride home I refused to talk to her and as soon as we got home I locked myself in the bathroom.

"Aidyn, it wasn't my idea to keep it from you," Mom hollered. I felt her weight on the other side of the door, felt her listening for any sound. "It's not so bad, is it? Nobody wanted to hurt you—"

"Go away! I'm just this dumb little sucker nobody wants around. I finally think *I'm* making friends, and I find out my *mommy* had to set it up." I sniffled and scrubbed my cheeks with the back of my hand. "I liked it better when I didn't know how stupid I am."

After that I ran the shower to drown her out, plunked on the cold toilet lid and smoldered. Why on earth should she worry about my trust, anyway? She'd never cared before. And why would Jackson care if I was mad at him? Why would anyone?

I picked at the chipped paint on the cabinet and wondered what Jackson would think if he knew how I was treating Mom. He and Elaine could just hate me more. But what about Shannon, or Lucy, or Miguel? What would they think and why should I care? But I did.

And they'd find out, because Mom was sure to call Elaine, and once again the whole bunch of them would discuss stupid little Aidyn, and Aidyn would be the only one left out.

I was so sick of being left out of my own life, most of the time.

I turned off the shower and wondered how I could make up with Mom without making it look like I thought she was right. I wondered if I should.

I thought of the scorn in Jackson's voice when he'd talked about Miguel. Did he really think I was that selfish? I didn't always think of myself!

Mom banged on the door. "Are you coming out, or do I have to drive myself to the gas station?"

I unlocked the door, and she brushed past me. "I'm going to a meeting this afternoon," she told me a few minutes later. "Elaine said something about going out for dinner afterward. I don't suppose you'd want to come?"

"I don't want to see Elaine."

After Mom left I wandered around the tiny apartment, as restless as she had been the week before. After all those years of spending time with myself I ought to be used to it, but the empty rooms shredded my soul. Raw and jumpy, I slammed out of the apartment and down the stairs. The Donaldsons were gone for the weekend, or I'd have offered to take the boys to the park. I decided I'd take myself there, anyway. Jackson and Miguel went there, after all.

But the weather had gotten blustery and only a few people braved the cold equipment. I kicked the end of the slide, gave a swing a push, and wished I were still young enough to get lost in dizziness. I might as well go home.

As bad as being with the youth group felt, I craved it. Craved their approval. And if they knew what kind of person I really was, I'd never get it. But how did I stop *not* talking to somebody, when I'd never had much practice?

Mom came home after I'd crawled in bed, and she didn't come to tell me good night. I missed it. I missed her. I got up and stood outside her bedroom door for what seemed like hours, but I couldn't make myself wake her. What excuse could I give?

The next day I ended up asking Miguel what he thought. He was different, like me, and he understood. He wouldn't blame me, would he? Or say everything was my fault?

I waited until he finished his lunch and headed toward the sports fields. Usually he joined the ongoing basketball game, but I got in his way and stammered, "Can I ask you something?"

"Sure." He studied me for a second before he jerked his head toward the garden area bedside the cafeteria. "What's up?"

I kept my head down. "I wanted to ask you…" I stopped. Why couldn't I get the question out? "My mom—she thinks I'm still mad at her."

"Have you tried talking to her?"

"Not exactly."

We reached the edge of the grass, and he stopped, studying the sky. "So, let's see. She thinks you're mad, and you haven't said you're not. That it?"

When he said it like that, I sounded a lot dumber than even I thought I was.

"And you're not sure how to talk to her, right?"

I was right. He *did* understand. I beamed at him. "Yeah."

He shrugged. "What can I tell you, Aidyn? I know what it's like. I was so scared of my mom for a long time but not nearly as scared of her as I was of my dad."

"I'm not really scared of her."

"Why not?"

"I—because!"

"So, you forgave her but you haven't told her yet."

"I guess."

"Well, here's the way I see it. You gotta tell her. Quick. Because you have other stuff you have to tell her. More important stuff."

"I do?"

"Well, yeah! You gotta tell her about me." He laughed, looked at me, and stopped. "Really. I mean that."

I stared up at him. So this thing I felt when I saw him, when he talked to me, was more than just recognition of a fellow hurting soul. We were more than that.

Still, I stammered, "What am I supposed to tell her?"

He tried to look offended, but he was grinning too hard for me to believe it. "What d'you think?"

"I think—I thought—we're friends."

"That's right. We are." And he reached out and took my hand. Though I only hoped I knew what he wanted me to tell Mom, I didn't care. He hadn't given me any advice I could chew up and turn into action, but that didn't matter, either. He had taken my hand and made everything fine.

"Hey, Miguel!" Jackson pounded up beside us. He gave me a short nod before he turned to Miguel, and I was just as glad, because my face flamed. "Shannon's getting everyone together to start the mural for the Autumn Dance. She says bring everybody."

Miguel turned to me. "You want to help paint?"

I shrugged. I would much rather stay out on the field with him, the two of us alone and exploring what our relationship might become, rather than tagging after him and standing on the outside of whatever group that included him. But Jackson dragged him toward the quad, and since Miguel still held my hand, I couldn't stay behind, even though I tried. "Miguel, I don't think I better help."

"Why not?"

I shook my head. "I don't…"

He waited for a second before tugging me toward the quad. "You don't what? Belong? Sure you do. We all do."

"Shannon doesn't want me to help."

"Shannon isn't the queen of the committee, you know."

That made me laugh. "You're wrong."

Maybe no one noticed. Maybe Jackson dragged reluctant outcasts into public at such regular intervals that no one cared, except for the outcast. I felt a million eyes glare at me, felt them wonder who I thought I was, what they'd have to do to get me to wise up and back off.

They could pick Shannon, former friend, fabulous traitor, as their leader.

Maybe they already had. She held court over a banner stretched like a beauty queen runway across the dirty concrete, held a paper plate in one hand and paintbrushes in the other. My mind flashed a picture of her trying to scoop enchiladas, or maybe birthday cake, into her mouth with sable bristles, before I saw the plate brimmed with an autumn flavored rainbow of glistening paint.

Paint. Brushes. Shannon and paint and that banner and me. The panic that had folded its wings during my confusion flared into flight and my feet stopped. Miguel, who hadn't halted, jerked my arm. Jackson jerked Miguel's and turned to check on the status of his train.

Once he'd tugged us into moving again, he said, "Aidyn, Shannon says you're an artist."

Once upon a time, maybe I had been. I didn't want to remember. I hadn't painted anything since my life spiraled out of normal. Even the art teachers who exploded with enthusiasm had never persuaded me to pick up another brush. Shannon didn't have a chance.

Still, she tried. "We need your help." She looked right into my face when she said that.

Rich, rich, rich. And when I needed her help, no, merely her friendship, when my life depended on the only friend I had, what had she done? I can learn by example as well as anyone else. Shannon taught me betrayal and desertion.

Shaking my head, I turned away. Into Jackson.

"Hey." He ringed my wrist with his fingers and pitched his voice so only I could hear. "That's no way to treat an old friend."

I stared into his ice-blue eyes, stricken. But he'd betrayed me, too.

"Aidyn." The one person I didn't resent whispered into my hair. "Come on. It's not that bad." The one person who could get to me when no one else had a chance. "We'll both help."

Next thing I knew I'd bowed to a pristine stretch of white banner, my own plate of traitorously beautiful paint in hand, my sable-bristled spoons ready to dish up humility for my soul.

I'd forgotten how I loved to paint. My fingers hadn't.

Shannon squatted next to me. "The theme is Harvest Sunshine. My idea. So we're doing all kinds of sun things. Sunflowers here in the middle. I remembered how your mom taught us how to paint them, but I was never any good at it, not like you. But as soon as we came up with this idea I told everyone about you, and I said you'd help."

Something in her voice tried to gloss over all the unsaid hurt and trembled at the edge of a lie. Part of me wanted to stare her down. Part of me craved what I'd have if I gave in. I could have a friend again, or at least, a semblance of one—illusion enough to fool the rest of the world into thinking me normal enough to deserve one. Or did I only want to fool myself?

Indecision is a great impetus, that, and people who grab your hand, help you dunk a paintbrush into a pool of gold, and start you on a journey back into the real world.

I painted sunflowers. Other than a slew of duds that could have been mud puddles as much as flowers, my nerves dipped into memory and came up with the beauty Shannon and the rest of the world demanded.

If only Miguel had stayed next to me. When I surfaced from the elation of my first perfect flower, he'd drifted far enough away that his jokes and clowning got lost in the crowd. I sighed and sank back on my heels. Beside me, Shannon used a detail brush to add tiny white specks to the flower centers that no one would see once they'd tacked the banner to the gym wall.

I wouldn't see any of it, of course. I'd never gone to a high school dance and didn't anticipate any in my future. What right did I have? No one wanted me there. I edged away from Shannon and started another still-sun-life. Shannon followed, dotting white onto my flowers, bits of light that illuminated nothing but my isolation.

"Aidyn." She leaned closer to me. "You're really good."

I shook my head. I was not good. I was so very not good. If she only knew.

She leaned even closer and pitched her voice lower still. "How's your mom doing?"

I looked up. "Mine?"

She nodded. "Is she still doing OK?"

"Yeah." I dropped the brush. "She quit drinking."

"I know. Jackson told me. I'm glad. Your mom is really nice, but it got so scary when—"

"When she was drunk." That word had become quite comfortable in my mouth.

"I wanted to tell you. I was at this party." Shannon stopped to move to yet another section, and I took her spot. "Not one of Lucy's, somewhere else. And they were drinking and stuff, and all I could think of was the look you used to get on your face when—well. So I called my mom and went home."

"Why?" Why the pity thing?

"Because I didn't…" She frowned at a stem which looked perfect to me. "I don't want you to get mad or anything. But I just didn't want to be like your mom. Not like she is now, but when she was…you know."

"Drunk."

She jerked her eyes to meet mine. "OK, yeah, when she was drunk. I knew how scared you always got, and I thought I would never want to do that to someone I loved—make them look that scared…that…defeated. You know?"

I closed my eyes before I answered. Why had I been so anxious to force Shannon to say the word I hated? Why did I ask her to beat me with it? "I don't, either. She wouldn't want you to, or me either, probably. She's not a drunk because she wants to be." Only after I said the words did I understand their truth.

"You should tell her that, then. She'd be glad." Shannon finished the last stem and slammed her brush down. "No, wait. I'll tell her myself. I don't have to listen to Mom all the time anymore. Can I come over after school?"

"To my apartment?" I sounded stupider than ever, but I couldn't help it. "I thought your mom…I mean, you said she's sick." Stupid and tactless, that was me.

Shannon shrugged and began to gather the dirty brushes. "We used to be best friends, Aidyn. But I got scared, and then…" Again she shrugged.

"Sure. You can come over." My heart pounded as I stood and helped to crumple the newspapers scattered across the concrete. First Miguel and then Shannon. And who else?

Jackson gave me a one-armed hug, holding his bucket of paint water out of my way. "This is the best mural we've ever had. Shannon was right. We need you."

9

Shannon and I had been at my house for almost half an hour before I realized the irony. I wouldn't talk to Mom, yet I planned to let Shannon talk to her? What would Mom think of that? I opened my mouth to explain, but I hate explaining anything. Even worse when the more I say, the worse I look. Besides, what could Shannon do but leave? For sure, she'd never try to talk to me again. And what if she told Jackson? He already thought I was a selfish baby. What would this make him think? No matter what I did now, I'd already sabotaged myself.

Maybe I could just act like Mom, like I'd never been mad, never ignored her, never behaved like a sulky five-year-old who has to always get her own way.

Mom got home before I could make any mistakes. She lugged in a stack of clay pots and gave Shannon a surprised, delighted look. "I'm glad there are two of you." She tucked the pots into a corner of the couch. "I've got a ton of very sick poinsettias in the car, and I could use some help bringing them up to the plant hospital here."

"Plant hospital?" Shannon followed Mom outside.

"My joke. I just can't stand to see those poor things die without trying to make them better."

We each made two trips before we got all the containers up to the apartment. Shannon and I lined them up on the kitchen counter while Mom stripped the cardboard to free the dirt and roots.

"These look like they're already dead." Shannon tried to prop an especially droopy flower on the faucet. "How long do you expect them to live?"

Mom shrugged. "Some will make it." She tipped the first one out and a rainy day, wet dirt smell filled the kitchen. "I just can't let it go, not do something."

"We were thinking of using poinsettias to decorate for our Christmas dance." Shannon curled her lip at the wilted, blood-colored leaves. "But now I don't think it's such a good idea."

Mom laughed and reached to stroke the petals. "Healthy plants look a lot better than this. Remember, these are about as bad as they can get."

Shannon nodded.

I pretended an interest in another carton while I studied the two of them from under my lashes. Shannon used to be great friends with my mom. She'd cried nearly as hard for my dad as I had. I felt my eyes fill up. I'd been so proud that my best friend cared so much about my parents because it proved how special they were.

"We painted the mural for Friday's dance today," Shannon told Mom. "Aidyn painted the coolest sunflowers all over it. Remember when you taught us how?"

Mom glanced at me, and I bent my head. "I do." She tapped soil from a plastic sack into one of the clay pots. "What dance is this?"

"Our harvest dance. Didn't Aidyn tell you about it?"

Mom gave me a longer look. "No, that hasn't come up."

I closed my eyes. How easy would it be for Mom to let Shannon know exactly how nasty I'd been the past few days? But Mom wasn't like that. Not when she was sober, and today she was.

Shannon turned to me. "I thought you wanted to go. Can she, Mrs. Pierce? She painted all those sunflowers for it." As if that were reason enough.

"Sure. You'd go as a group, right? The youth group?" Mom hesitated over the last words, as if she suspected I'd flame up and incinerate her for mentioning them.

"Oh, yeah, we always go together. We watch each other's backs, you know? 'Cause it can be really easy to get caught up in all the drinking and drugs and stuff. I mean, one time—"

Mom nodded. I still hadn't said anything. Had Shannon noticed?

"This one time," Shannon went on, "I went to a party with my cousin. That's why I came today, because I thought I should tell you. I told Aidyn, and I thought you'd want to know, too. There was all this drinking going on at this party, and my cousin thought that was so cool."

Mom set down the pot and turned to face Shannon, her hands on the counter behind her, arms tense.

"But it reminded me of Aidyn, you know? Not the drinking. Aidyn'd *never* do that. But because I remembered how much she hated it when you'd...well, you know. And...and I didn't want to do that to someone else...make them feel the way she felt—all miserable and scared all the time." Her voice trailed off. I think Mom's lack of enthusiasm got through to Shannon, and she faltered.

"You know, because when you'd...well, sometimes I thought Aidyn—I thought she'd die. I thought she wanted to, I mean. I used to beg my mom to let me bring her home to live with us."

I'd never heard that. I watched Mom, still backed up to the counter, her eyes closed now, swaying slightly.

Shannon's foot jiggled. "So I thought you might want to know that...that I'll never dri...you know, because I don't ever want to make someone else feel like that."

Mom walked out of the kitchen, trailing bits of soil from her fingers. I heard her bedroom door slam. I stared at the dirt scattered across the counter and spilling into the sink, and the lone plant with its wasted roots thrusting out of the packed soil.

"I guess...I guess she didn't like to hear that."

"No."

"I better go now. I'm sorry, Aidyn. I really am." Her voice rose with her anguish, and it was like hearing a ghost from the past crying with me again. "I didn't mean to hurt her feelings."

She watched me for long minutes before she checked her cell phone. "Mom's gonna be mad enough. I better not miss helping her fix dinner. You want Jackson and me to pick you up for the dance? We can get Miguel, too."

"I don't know." I brushed some of the dirt off the counter into my cupped palm. "He didn't say anything about going."

"He told Jackson he wanted to go with you."

My heart lifted out of its slough for one glorious moment and plummeted again. "I guess he forgot to tell me." I glanced at the hallway leading to Mom's room.

"Yeah, well, I better go." Shannon collected her backpack and let herself out. I stood with a fistful of dirt in front of the sink. Shannon poked back in. "Aidyn, tell your mom…I mean, she's really cool, when she's not…you know. I really like her."

I nodded and squeezed the soil into a muddy lump in my sweaty palm while I listened to Shannon clang down the metal staircase.

I walked to the middle of the living room and froze. Should I knock on Mom's door and let her know Shannon had gone? I thought of calling Elaine and asking her to call Mom. I wondered if Mom had anything hidden away in her room. When I was younger I knew all her hiding places, but I'd given up dumping everything I could find. Now, I didn't know. What if…?

Before I could decide on anything, Mom stalked into the kitchen. She attacked the poinsettias as though she were into mercy killing, breaking stems and slamming squishy root packets into the pots.

I edged past her and rinsed my hands. "I'm sorry, Mom. I never said anything to her. Never."

"I'm sure you didn't. Maybe it would have been better if you had."

I stared at her, perplexed.

Mom shook her head. "Aidyn, did the whole world know what I was doing to you? She did—a little kid! Everyone knew but me, and no one bothered to tell me." She rubbed her face, leaving chunks of mud and tendrils of root across her cheeks. "Listen to me. Putting all the responsibility on everyone else."

She grabbed a paper towel and scrubbed her face.

I let warm water flow over my hands, sure that

A Fistful of God

when I turned off the tap I'd say the wrong thing again.

"Aidyn, I wish I could tell you that if only someone had told me how much harm I was doing to you, I would have quit right then. But that's not true." She slumped against the counter. "I hate being an alcoholic."

I turned off the faucet and stared at my water-wrinkled hands, then looked over at Mom. She'd stopped working again and stood with her arms crossed, her shoulders thin and shaking under her sweater.

"But you quit."

"Finally."

I wiped my hands over and over on my jeans. "I heard you talking on the phone. Maybe to Elaine. Sunday."

She looked up.

"You said you quit for"—I could only mouth the word—"me."

She nodded.

I looked up at her. "That's the truth?"

"The absolute truth, baby. Who else do I love as much as I love you?"

I tried to find something to say and couldn't. Mom wrapped her arms around me and leaned her face against the top of my head.

"I'm sorry Shannon embarrassed you. She didn't mean to. She thought you'd...I don't know. I guess she thought you'd like to know you'd done some good."

Mom snorted. "And I used to dream what a great role model I'd be."

"She thinks you're cool. She told me to say so."

Mom backed away. "Well, you know better, don't

you?"

"Mom, sometimes you're cool. Yeah, lately...Mom?" A tear trickling down her cheek cut my heart. "Mom, I'm sorry I didn't believe you when you said you were going to quit. I'm sorry I didn't think you could."

She shook her head. "I've never been very good at keeping that promise, have I?"

"But you are," I said. "You're keeping it."

"For today." Again she leaned into me, and I hugged her back. She didn't smell like booze or even Elaine's putrid perfume, but like potting soil and laundry detergent and something else I couldn't name but took me back to the days when we'd been friends—days when I lived in a safe world.

I started to cry. "I used to pray so hard you'd quit, and it never did any good. So I just gave up. I mean, if God couldn't make you, who could?"

"Oh, baby," Mom choked.

"And then, when you did, and you didn't start again, I started asking Him to keep everything good."

"So have I, baby. So have I."

For two weeks I lived my life like a fairytale. As if I'd just noticed how perfect life could be without a drunk in it, I floated into friendships with Mom, with Shannon, with Miguel. I could even tolerate Elaine, and she seemed to hate me a bit less, too. I bounced around my world like a child delighted in life. For the first time I felt free.

On Friday evening, Jackson picked up the three of us early. I gave Mom a quick hug, reminded her to call Elaine if she needed to, and raced down the stairs. This would be the first time Miguel and I went out together, and even though he hadn't said it was a date, I knew it was. What else could it be?

After our third dance, Miguel led me to the area set aside for the punch and cookies. "Are you hungry already?" I teased. "What happened to that dinner you told me you ate?"

He grinned. "I just wanted to get away from the speakers."

I nodded. "We don't have to yell as loud here." I looked down at my hands, clutched together.

"Aidyn." He paced away and then back. Over his shoulder I saw a group of seniors surround the refreshments table. "What do you think of us?"

We were an "us"? Could the world get any better? "I think—you said we're friends."

"I think I did, too." He grinned. "But some of the guys—oh, Wallis and them—they think...they say because we're always together that we're...together. You know?"

I nodded.

"So I was wondering." He looked away, biting his lip. I wanted so badly to give him the words, or the courage, whatever it was he needed to be able to say what I needed to hear. I lay my hand on his arm and he looked down at me. "Why don't we just...we could say we are together. If you want to."

Again I nodded.

"Good." He bent his head, and his lips barely brushed mine.

The seniors roared, and we sprang apart, but they were laughing at some joke of their own, not at us. Still, Miguel jerked his head in the direction of the main hall. "Come on, Aidyn. We'd better go dance, OK?"

I wished I could tell him that anything he wanted

would be OK with me, but I didn't have any courage of my own.

The next Friday Mom let Miguel take me on our first two-of-us date. His mom drove us to the local street fair, and we walked the rows of booths. Neither of us had much money, and it didn't matter. We had each other, and enough, Miguel said, to get ourselves some dessert.

"We don't need it, Miguel." I held his hand, my shoulder pressed close to his arm. "We don't need anything else."

Smoke from a barbecue drifted through the stalls. I couldn't tell when it got dark because of the blaring lights. The place felt like a carnival, crowds moving and bumping us, not seeing us but still a part of us. The scents of popcorn and roasted, sugared pecans, chocolate, and french-fries wafted in the air. A country western band played, interrupted by the sounds of laughter, a kid crying, and the hiss of a helium tank. All around were painted wood and blown glass, hand-sewn dresses, and handmade jewelry.

"Look at these." Miguel pulled me toward a booth. A hodgepodge of silver dragons and wizards, crystal balls clutched in tiny silver claws and earrings spilled out of wooden trays and across crumpled turquoise silk. Miguel pointed to a case of necklaces. "Did you see the crosses? You said you wanted one, didn't you?"

I had. Most of the girls and a lot of the guys in the youth group wore one. I wanted one, just to prove I belonged.

"This one." He pointed again and the woman working the booth unlocked the case and lifted it out. "How much? I've got fifteen dollars." He grinned at me. "If you don't mind skipping the ice cream."

"I don't mind. But Miguel, I don't want you to spend all your money on me."

"I do."

"Oh, Miguel—"

"Sorry," the woman said as she laid the chain over Miguel's palm. "This one is twenty. It's made with a special procedure called the 'lost wax' method. I make the mold from wax, pour in the silver and as it sets the wax is melted, or lost. Makes for a one-of-a-kind design." She smiled and waved for me to take a closer look. Dull, like pewter, a tiny rose grew from the base and bloomed in the center.

Miguel turned to me, stricken. "I don't have that much. I'm sorry, Aidyn, if I could—"

"That's OK, really."

"Look at me," the woman said.

I turned to her. "What?"

She tipped my chin up and lifted my glasses to stare into my eyes. Her face blurred, but I could still sense the way she studied me. Her eyes were so light a color they seemed to be light themselves. I thought she must be crazy—sincere, but crazy. I wanted to pull away so she couldn't learn everything there was to know about me, but I kept myself from flinching.

"I can see it in your eyes. You're good people. I'll let you have it for fifteen, all right?" She let go.

"But..." I backed away, spluttering.

"Don't worry about it, honey. I wouldn't do this if it wasn't a cross, but I can see you love what it stands for. You're a good person; you deserve this."

Miguel handed over all his money and clasped the chain around my neck. I stood, wooden, sure I'd cheated her. As Miguel thanked her I felt the cross at my throat, felt the rose and tucked my nail under the edge of its stem.

"Are you sure?" I asked before Miguel could lead me away. "It's not right—"

"There's right and then there's right." She slipped the money into a box. "I've had that one for months and never found anyone I wanted to have it more. You need it, don't you?"

Not want, but need. I knew the difference, and still, I nodded.

She smiled. "You're good people." Then she turned to another customer.

I had no choice but to follow Miguel to where we'd agreed to meet his mother. I'd wear the necklace every day, I swore to myself. And I knew, whenever I said "Thank You" to God, I'd reach up and stroke my tiny rose.

10

Jackson, Miguel, and I huddled at the back of the church hall, waiting for Lucy to start the meeting. I peered over Miguel's shoulder, hoping to see Shannon. If she knew the two of them had ambushed me, she'd come to my rescue. But she hadn't come in yet, and no one else in the crowded hall paid any attention to the three of us. I was stuck arguing my way out.

"You should go," Jackson said.

"It doesn't hurt." That was from Miguel.

I raised one eyebrow at him. He had no idea what might hurt. "It's not like I need to go."

Jackson's jaw dropped. "How can you say that? I know kids whose parents have been sober a lot longer than my mom, and they still go. They still need the support."

"Well, I don't. OK?"

Why the need to lie? I *knew* the truth, and yet all I could do was lock it away until it burned a hole through my soul, until it blazed on my face like a badge of admission, until the others knew just as well as I did—maybe better—that I couldn't allow myself to dance with the truth.

Miguel shrugged, his head down and his elbows braced on his knees. "What are you gonna do if your mom starts drinking again?"

"She won't!" That time quite a few turned to look. I lowered my voice, but it rasped with the effort. "She won't. I know my mom."

I don't *live* a lie; I *am* a lie.

"Don't tell me she promised you she wouldn't."

I glared at Jackson, at his eyes ice blue with anger, his taut jaw. "Of course not. But I know her."

"She's like any other alcoholic—"

"She is not! Don't you say that, Miguel! She's not like your dad." I couldn't even stop the lies for the one person on the world I knew I loved.

Miguel got up, but Jackson grabbed his arm. "She's honeymooning. Remember? Let her get it out of her system."

"You don't understand." But I was the one who didn't.

Jackson interrupted. "I do. Miguel and I both understand better than you do. Look, Aidyn, your mom's sober, and that's great. And she might be one of the lucky ones who never takes another drink. I don't know. But there are plenty of other issues you need to work through."

"Everything's fine with Mom and me. Perfect."

"Hey, guys, want to join us?" Lucy called over the PA, and I got my reprieve.

But I pressed against Miguel's side during the opening prayer and whispered, "I'm sorry. I shouldn't have said that about your dad."

He grunted, but after a bit he took my hand, and I knew everything was OK between us. If only he'd held it before, I'd have felt his strength run into me through his warm, cinnamon skin. I'd have been safe. I wouldn't have had to lie.

Lucy's message that day centered on thankfulness. "Maybe I should wait for Thanksgiving, right? It's only a month away, and then I'd be in season. But the thing is, we always have something to be thankful for. We ought to be thankful every single day we're alive, just for the simple fact that we *are* alive. And then we go from there. We, each of us, have so many reasons to thank the Lord. We need to thank Him for the good things, the feasts, as well as for the bad things, the times when the feasts are going on but we're not invited. We are called to be thankful in *everything*."

She waved her arms to include the whole world in her everything. I grinned to myself. I could do thankful. I'd come through the time of not being invited, and now I held my own feast.

Later, when Miguel sneaked back to grab another handful of cookies off the snack table, Lucy stopped next to me.

"I really liked what you said about being thankful," I told her.

She nodded. "You look so happy these days. I'm glad. I guess you have a lot to thank Him for right now." She glanced toward Miguel, and I grinned. "Keep it, Aidyn. Remember this when you think you have nothing to be thankful for."

Miguel and I walked to my apartment holding hands, and the whole way I kept my other hand on my silver cross. Whenever I thought about it, I thanked God. I would go on thanking Him, and I would always be able to, because I knew there would never come another time when it seemed all my blessings had been taken away.

****

The Saturday before Halloween I convinced Miguel to give up his teen support meeting to help me help Mrs. Donaldson get her boys ready for trick-or-treating. Lucas wanted to be Batman, and Andy insisted he wanted to be exactly the same as Lucas, who didn't like that idea at all.

While the four of us carved pumpkins, crowded in the Donaldson's kitchen with newspapers thick under our knees, we tried to convince Lucas that Andy could be Batman, or convince Andy that he could be something else.

Miguel dropped a glop of pumpkin innards onto the papers. "My little brother was just like Andy. Always copying me, you know? I hated it. Thought he was a real pain in the butt."

Mrs. Donaldson turned from her dinner preparations to give Miguel a glare of disapproval, and he returned it with one of his more angelic smiles. She shook her head but didn't stop him.

"But I thought about it a long time. Here was this little kid—he was just about Andy's size then—and he wanted to be everything I was. *Everything*. Man, the things I could get him to do!"

Mrs. Donaldson glared at Miguel. "Like clean your room?"

"Well, no." Miguel leaned away from her. I pressed the back of my slimy hand to my mouth to keep from laughing out loud. "I wasn't too interested in clean rooms, Mrs. Donaldson. But I wanted to be a superhero. Like you, Lucas. And I finally figured something out."

Miguel settled cross-legged again and held his hand out for the knife. "I figured out that I was already a hero to my little brother. No matter what, that kid loved everything I did. I could be a hero no matter what day it was, or how I dressed up."

Mrs. Donaldson nodded, but she went on watching Miguel. He bent over the pumpkin, cleaning the edge of the opening with short, smooth strokes.

Lucas sighed. "Andy wants to *be* me."

Miguel looked up. "Feels kinda good, doesn't it?"

Lucas nodded. Not too long after that, he told his mom she could make Andy a black cape. "But it has to be shorter than mine, because he's not as big as me."

After we got the kitchen cleaned up and Mrs. Donaldson thanked us and paid us extra, as usual, Miguel and I sat at the top of the stairs, waiting for Mom to get home.

Miguel started to laugh. "I thought Mrs. Donaldson was gonna carve me up with her baby pumpkin knife."

"She's pretty picky about what the boys are exposed to. She doesn't want them to think it's OK to *not* clean your room." He leaned against my knee. "I didn't know you had a little brother."

"I don't." He stared across the apartment courtyard. "I was talking about my older brother. He was my hero, Aidyn. Until he died on that stupid motorcycle, I wanted to be just like him."

I heard the pain in his voice. "You're not."

"I don't want to be like my dad, either. I'm gonna be strong, like my mom." He laughed. "No, I'm gonna be Batman."

"You'll be strong. Even if you're scared, you'll be strong when you need to be."

****

The afternoon before Halloween, Mr. Donaldson called me. "Margie has the flu, and I don't really want to leave her. But we promised the boys we'd take them out. Do you think you and Miguel could take them? They'd be home early enough for the two of you to go to a party or whatever you had planned."

"I'm not sure if Miguel will want to." But I knew how attached he'd gotten to those boys. My ploy worked. Mr. Donaldson promised to pay double, and I called Miguel to tell him we had a job.

After we got the boys home, cleaned up, roughhoused enough to tire them out so they could sleep after the candy we let them eat, Miguel and I went back to my apartment. Mom sat with her feet up, reading one of her thousands of library books. "Help yourselves to some candy," she said. "I've got almost a whole bag left. Hardly anybody stopped here. I heard the kids on the stairs, but they'd just run right by."

Panicked, I stared at Miguel. *I* knew why they hadn't stopped. They remembered last year, when Mom would yank open the door and scream at anybody who rang the bell. I turned and, making sure Miguel stood between my hand and Mom, I flipped the porch light off.

"You forgot the light, Mom. We thought you must have run out of candy and turned it off." Because wasn't it better to lie than to make her feel bad? Somehow, I couldn't imagine Lucy or one of the priests at church, or even Mom, agreeing with me.

Mom frowned. "I'm sure I—" She shrugged. "I must have forgotten."

I tried to think back. Even after Miguel's mom picked him up and Mom and I had gone to bed, I lay in the dark, trying to make things come out right. Had Mom forgotten, blacked out as long ago as a year? Had it gotten that bad by then? Sour fear crept into my stomach. I *didn't* want to remember times like those. I wanted to hold Mom's sobriety to me, as close as I could, and never have to think about the past again.

Shaking, I clutched my silver cross. "Thank You that it's over. Help me forget all that."

****

I guess God didn't want me to forget, because a few days later Mom staggered through the apartment door, collapsed on the couch and huddled over her lap. I stood in the kitchen doorway, feeling my whole life guzzled away. Mom had dropped her purse on the floor and I didn't see any bottles but that didn't mean she didn't have one clutched to her heart. It didn't mean she hadn't already finished the whole thing off.

"Mom?"

"Aidyn?" She turned to me, wincing. "I have the worst headache." She sighed. "I've had hangovers this bad, but not often."

"Do you want something?"

She shook her head. "No. I think I just need to sleep." But she stayed on the couch. "My stomach hurts, too. I should have stopped and gotten some ginger ale. That might have helped."

"Do you want me to go get some?"

"Do you mind? I'd appreciate that."

So I ended up walking three blocks to get a six-pack of soda for her stomach and thinking mine needed it just as badly.

When I got back I asked, "What's for dinner?"

"I don't know. Can't you just open a can of soup?"

I backed away. "Yeah, I guess. What kind do you want?"

"I'm not hungry." She poured a glass of ginger ale and lay back on the couch. Even when I brought a bowl of chicken soup to her, she didn't want it. I put it in the fridge and stared at my tiny pile of dishes. Nothing had changed, had it? Mom was drunk and trying to hide it. Just because I couldn't see it or smell it didn't change anything. Pretty soon she'd pass out, and my nightmare would suck me into its rancid mouth and swallow me whole. But it couldn't, because I wasn't whole.

I tiptoed into the room. Her eyes were closed, her breathing heavy. No snoring, like when she was really drunk, but—

I knelt next to her. "Mom, I think you better go to a meeting."

She jerked like I'd woken her. "Not tonight, OK?'

Biting my lip, I got up. I'd given her another chance. She could have decided to go. I washed my dishes and finished my homework and spent a lot of time holding onto my cross. *Please don't let it start again. Please!* And underneath my prayers ran the mantra—too late, too late.

And here I'd convinced myself Mom went to those meetings three times a week because she had so many friends there.

I headed for the living room and turned on the TV. Mom sat up, dragging her hair off her face. "Can't you turn that down?"

I did, but after a few minutes she stirred again. "Do you have to have that on?"

"Why don't you go to a meeting?" I muttered. "Then I could do what I want without you bagging on me."

"I don't feel like it, OK? I told you that."

A Fistful of God

I switched off the TV and stared at the empty screen. I touched my cross, but it felt just as empty. Mom sat up and reached for her glass.

"What are you drinking?"

"Ginger ale. You bought it, remember?"

I shook my head. She'd sneaked something else into it. She had to have. And I knew why she wouldn't go to a meeting. She'd quit quitting, and why would she go when she'd decided to drink?

I turned off all but one light and crept to my room. A long time later I heard her stumble to the bathroom. I heard her heaving and gasping, the splash of vomit on the tiles. At least it hadn't hit the carpet. I clenched every muscle in my body and hated her. It would have been so much better to never have hoped. I thought she called me, but I pretended not to hear.

I hadn't taken the cross off since Miguel fastened it around my neck, but I sat up then and undid the clasp. Shaking, I threw it at the wall. "Why? I believed in You. I trusted You. So why?"

Mom called again, threw up again, and I fell asleep crying.

In the morning, my head felt stuffed like I'd injected pillow fluff under my skin. When I got up I found Mom sprawled in the hall just outside the bathroom door. The apartment reeked of vomit. I swallowed. How many times had she missed?

"Get up." I grabbed her arm and jerked her up, but she could barely stand.

"Call Toni. I'm sick."

She staggered against me, stumbled as I pulled her into her room. I pushed her as roughly as I could onto the bed. "I know better than to believe you're sick."

I cleaned the bathroom and the soiled carpet,

gagging as I lugged the dirty towels to the laundry room. I jammed in the coins and started the washer, then headed back to the apartment.

"Aidyn." Mom's voice came weak and hoarse.

Bad hangover, I thought, although I wasn't sure she had reached that stage yet. She still acted drunk; she probably was.

I leaned on the doorjamb and glared at her.

"Call Toni. Tell her I have the flu."

"I'm calling her right now." I punched in Toni's work number. "It's Aidyn. Mom won't be in to work today. She's got a hangover."

Toni swore.

"I wasn't drinking." Mom hitched up on one elbow and reached for the phone, but I danced out of her way. "I swear, Aidyn. I've got the flu."

"Yeah, she was really drunk last night. I think she still is."

"I don't need this," Toni said.

"You think I do?" I slammed the phone, making sure Mom couldn't reach it from the bed. But that wasn't good enough. I've known her to call a liquor store for another delivery when she couldn't walk, so I grabbed the cord and yanked it from the wall.

"Aidyn, I wasn't drinking. I promise."

I slammed her door and the front door as loud as I could when I left.

11

I ran downstairs and hid in the laundry room and felt eleven again. That's how old I was when I first realized Mom's drinking wasn't ever going to stop, that my life would never go back to the way it had been when Daddy was alive. I slammed the basket down on the lid of an empty washer and slammed my fist against the metal then I curled up between two dryers and hated myself for trusting her again. Why did she have to drink? Why did I have to get so mad?

"Don't break the washer," Lucas said and I jumped.

Mrs. Donaldson maneuvered through the door with Andy on one hip and a basket of dirty clothes on the other. She'd want to know why I wasn't in school, but she couldn't make me go. No one could make me face Jackson and Miguel and admit they'd been right and I'd been wrong.

"You OK, Aidyn?" Mrs. Donaldson looked almost scared to ask me.

"Yeah." I tried to keep the surliness from my voice, but I lost the battle. I'd lost every battle lately.

She raised her eyebrows then sighed. "I saw your mom's car. Is she home today, too?"

I scrambled to my feet and stalked out, leaving my basket of nasty towels on top of the dryer. Did *everyone* have to know? Mrs. Donaldson probably thought I was as stupid and childish as Miguel and Jackson did because I believed my perfect little fantasy could last forever. It hadn't even lasted a month.

I crept through the courtyard to the street, but I was scared to go any farther. I hardly ever ditched but if I did today, for sure I'd get caught, and what would happen when the cops called my mom to find out why? Well, they'd find out fast. That was sure.

After watching the street, though, I gathered up enough courage to run around the corner to the thrift store, my haven. I could sit in the back and spend hours going through the paperbacks. The lady who ran the store didn't care who was there as long as we didn't make trouble for her. I knew how to not make trouble.

I didn't trudge home until I realized I'd missed both breakfast and lunch. The apartment door was shut and locked. I remembered slamming it, but not locking it. Mom must have gotten up. Had she opened the door for a delivery? I bit my lip. I should have stayed home. I'd have turned the delivery away and then maybe she'd have been able to stop again. But now?

Inside I sniffed. No wine, just a lingering sourness and the cleaner I'd used on the floors. I heard Mom's voice, saying, "No, no, that's all." She must have been able to get up to plug in the phone. I wondered who she'd called. Joyce? Elaine? Or for another delivery?

Toni walked out of the hall and caught me shaking in the middle of the living room. "Aidyn!" She stepped back to call, "She's back, Beth." The scowl she turned on me puzzled me.

"What are you doing here?" I glared as hard at Mom's boss as she did at me, but tension uncurled in my stomach, and I thought I'd be just as sick as Mom.

"Aidyn," Mom called, but I ignored her.

"We just got back from the hospital." Toni shifted and crossed her arms. "They had to put an IV in her; she'd gotten so dehydrated. But she kept down some soup so I guess she's getting better."

I blinked at the soup bowl in her hand. "Why'd you take her there? It's just a hangover."

"It just isn't." Toni gave me the kind of look she used to keep for Mom, disgusted and irritated. "If you'd listened to your mother for once, I wouldn't have had to leave the nursery to come take care of her."

She handed me the bowl, and I set it on the coffee table. "What are you talking about?"

"Your mother. Who has the flu, which she told you."

"She wasn't drinking?" I stared at Toni without seeing much of her face, only her eyes burning into mine, full of accusations. If only I'd believed Mom. If only I'd trusted her. If only I hadn't left her when she was sick. But I'd hurt her again, for nothing. I dodged around Toni and bolted into Mom's room.

She lay on her side, one hand dangling over the edge, her hair damp with sweat and flattened against her white face.

I squatted next to her, my fingertips on the mattress. "Mom?"

"Aidyn." She didn't open her eyes, but she reached for me. "Baby, where'd you go?"

"The thrift store. Mom, I'm sorry. I should have believed you. I should've known you wouldn't lie to me."

"No." She swallowed, and when I stroked her cheek, she opened her eyes. "If I had been drinking, you can bet I would have lied to you about it."

"No, Mom."

"Sure, I would. I always have, haven't I? That wouldn't..." she sighed. "That wouldn't change. Don't feel bad, baby. Toni's mad, but I don't blame you at all."

She nestled deeper into the pillow, her eyelids fluttering shut. I rolled to my knees and watched her breathe. "Mom, can I get you anything?"

"No." She waved her fingers. "Toni made me eat, and I just need to sleep. I'm OK, as long as you're here..." Her voice trailed off.

"I won't leave again." I crept back to the living room.

Toni had cleaned up the kitchen, and I could tell she'd done it not to help out but to give herself a reason to stay and chew me out. Her glare made me feel four years old again, and very bad.

"You didn't have to act like that. You weren't being fair, were you? And I called and called and got no answer so I came over. Lucky thing I did, too!"

"I told her I was sorry." I was not going to tell Toni that, though.

"Well, all I can say is you'd better not tell me that again unless you know it's true. The first time I called was to tell Beth she was fired."

"I won't tell you anything."

She stared at me, her lip curling, and I sneered back. I sure didn't want my attitude to lose Mom her job, but Toni could really get on my nerves.

She finally leaned to pick up her purse, but as she slung it over her shoulder she told me, "You don't deserve her, Aidyn."

"What?"

"I know living with an alcoholic isn't any picnic, but Beth would do anything for you. She'd die for you. And you treat her like crap."

"I don't—"

"You're just a selfish, spoiled brat and the sooner she figures that out, the better off she'll be." She left me shaking again, trying to hold the shock inside me. Toni couldn't be right, not about everything. Not about me. What right did she have to walk in here and judge me? After all, my mother forgave me.

I eased Mom's door open without squeaking the hinges so I could listen to her breathing. In between cleaning and folding laundry, I stood outside her door and watched her—watched her chest rise and fall. I savored the grace of the moment when I'd realized Mom hadn't started drinking again. The whole miserable day had been my fault. I was stupid and selfish and undeserving, just as Toni said, but I could deal with that. I could deal with anything but Mom drinking.

When the phone rang, I dashed to grab it before it woke her.

"Where were you today?" Miguel asked.

"Home. Mom has the flu, and she ended up in the hospital. But she's home now."

"Don't you get sick, OK? I missed you, Aidyn."

"I missed you, too."

"You coming to school tomorrow?"

"Yeah, I think so. I mean, unless Mom is a lot worse."

"I need to see you, Aidyn."

Surprise kept me silent.

"Aidyn?"

"I'm here. Why? What's wrong?"

"Nothing. My dad. Talk about being worse."

"Mom is sick!" How dare he assume it was booze that made her sick.

But that's what I'd done.

"And my dad isn't." His voice roughened. "Only he keeps telling me it's a disease, but that's only when he's trying to get sober. It's evil, is what it is."

"Did he hit you again?"

A long silence, and then, "Yeah. Just the one time, though, so I didn't tell Mom. Not like any cop is gonna come out for that, anyway. You know? They're gonna look at me and wonder why such a big guy can't take a little smacking around."

"Did you tell him to stop?"

"Yeah. Much good that did. He laughed." Miguel choked on the hate. "The bully laughed at me when I told him to leave me alone."

"Oh, Miguel! I wish—if Mom didn't need me I'd walk to your house."

"I know." The longing in his voice wrenched my heart, and all I wanted was the chance to hold him while he cried.

After we said good-bye, I found my cross, put it on and made a fist around it. "You helped me." I traced the tiny rose with my thumbnail. "Now help Miguel. Don't let him get hurt. Don't let his dad get to him anymore."

Mom stayed home the rest of the week, and when she could work, she went only for a few hours. Even that wore her out, and each afternoon I'd tiptoe into the apartment, listen to her breathe, and tell myself she wasn't drunk.

By Friday she'd improved enough to work a full day and to drop Miguel and me at the street fair. "I'll

A Fistful of God

be here at nine," she reminded me before she drove off.

I leaned into the window. "Bye, Mom. Thanks."

I turned and let Miguel capture my hand with his large, warm fingers. I traced a familiar scar-ridge with my thumb. I only wanted to find someplace quiet and private, a place where we could become each other's safety, each other's world, a place where the cold of fear could never intrude.

"Where to?" Miguel asked.

"I've got all my babysitting money with me. I want to find the silver lady again. I'm going to buy a cross for Mom."

"Gee, I wish you'd buy me some ice cream." He dragged me in the direction of The Big Scoop.

"Later." I pulled against him and even though he's miles taller than me, he let me tow him through the crowds.

But we couldn't find her. "Creepy," I said. "She was creepy when we bought my cross, and now it's even weirder."

"I think she was an angel," Miguel said. "She knew you needed a cross so she was here that day, just for you."

"Then she ought to know Mom needs a cross." I peered along the lines of stalls.

"Aidyn?"

I turned, met Toni's glare. After I introduced her to Miguel as "Mom's boss," which told him all he needed to know of my opinion of her, she asked, "Where's your mother? You didn't leave her alone, did you?"

"She went to a meeting."

Toni nodded. "I just hope you take better care of her from now on."

After she'd stalked past us, Miguel made faces at her back. "She's crazy. You're not the mother. It's not your job to look after anybody."

I wondered, though. Things went so much smoother when I took control.

He poked me. "I want my ice cream now. You promised."

"One scoop." But I let him choose two and extra toppings.

As we came out of the shop, Miguel hollered, "Hey, Jackson!" He whooped, waved his cone like a lasso, and loped across the street.

I followed him. Jackson had stopped, but something about the way he looked at Miguel, and about the way he let Shannon hang on his arm, made me wonder exactly how glad he'd been to hear Miguel call him.

"I didn't know you guys were coming here," Miguel said. "Now we got someone to hang out with."

"For a while, I guess," Jackson said. "Where you guys headed?"

"Nowhere," I told him, as Miguel said, "Wherever you're going."

Shannon giggled, tugged on Jackson's arm, and whispered something. He made a face and that was when I noticed the smudges next to his mouth, which matched Shannon's wiped-off-looking lipstick.

"Let's go in here." I spun Miguel into a Chinese restaurant and watched Jackson and Shannon hesitate then wander off.

"What was that all about?" Miguel demanded. "What's wrong with spending time with friends?"

"They wanted to be alone."

"How do you know?"

"Did they follow us in here?" I asked, just as a waiter bounded up brandishing menus.

"Table for two?"

"No." Miguel glared at me. "Not unless you have some sort of special for crazy people."

The waiter had been so eager to seat us he probably would have promised a straitjacket if it came with egg rolls, but we scurried out.

"I don't get you, Aidyn." Miguel stomped beside me, fists in his pockets, not even trying to hold my hand.

Our first fight, and it wasn't even about us. I stomped away.

"Aidyn, wait up."

I stopped, embarrassed.

"I didn't mean to make you mad. I just wanted to hang with them."

"It's their date, Miguel. We can't just tag along."

"Yeah, well, I thought we ought to save them from themselves, you know?"

"Why?" I peered at him in the growing dark. "They like each other, but it looks like you're trying to break them up. Are you still trying to get Shannon to go out with you?"

"No! Aidyn, no. I just...they were...you know."

"And you wanted to what, watch?"

"No." He started to walk, but after a second he took my hand and held it close to his side. We wandered toward the park, found it overflowing with kids and walked even farther, to the empty bandstand. Miguel hitched himself up and reached a hand down for me. I huddled next to him, kicking my heels against the platform, wondering. Something skittered in the shadows behind us and I shivered.

"Are you cold?" Miguel leaned back, his arm stretched behind me, not touching.

With him so close? "No." But maybe he wanted me to be cold.

"Aidyn?" he whispered, much closer than I'd thought. "What would you do—I mean, do you ever…" He took a deep breath, and the sweetness left over from the ice cream brushed my cheek. "Sometimes I start thinking I'm seeing you for the last time. Like, if there's anything I want to tell you, I have to tell you now. Do you ever feel like that?"

I shook my head.

"Sometimes I get scared, Aidyn."

"So do I."

We turned at the same time, and his mouth feathered against my cheek, against my lips. He held my arm, his hand warm and solid, and kissed me again.

"Oh, Miguel." I opened my eyes. I couldn't see anyway so I took my glasses off. "Miguel, don't be scared. Neither one of us is going away."

He answered with a third kiss. A long time later I looked at my watch and yelped. Even though we ran to the other end of the street fair, we were half an hour late meeting Mom.

I went to sleep late that night, exhausted, exhilarated, in trouble for being late, and in the morning I woke up with the flu.

12

Until Sunday night I couldn't think of anything other than how bad it hurt to throw up. Mom spent as much time checking on my sleep as I had on hers, and when I finally woke without aches and cramps, she came in and perched on the edge of my bed.

"You're looking better." She swept the hair from my forehead. "I brought some fresh tea."

I moaned and turned away.

"I know. I didn't want to put anything in my stomach, either."

She left and came back a few minutes later with a red rosebud in her best crystal vase. I gasped as she set it on my desk. "It's perfect." Roses, even one tiny bud, cost so much in November. "Did Miguel bring it?"

"No." Mom crawled onto the end of my bed and sat cross legged close to my feet. "I asked Toni to bring it for you. She just left."

"Oh, OK. It's beautiful." I tried to smile. "Thanks, Mom."

She stared at her hands, and I realized I hadn't been very gracious. "Mom, I'm sorry. It's not that I don't like it because you gave it to me."

"I know."

"I didn't mean to hurt your feelings."

"You didn't, baby. There's something else." Her silence scared me. She covered my knee and massaged it through my blankets. Even without my glasses, I realized how bad she looked, like she had the flu herself all over again, or like she'd just stopped drinking.

My stomach cramped again. "What's wrong?"

"Jackson called. We weren't at Mass, and he wanted to know if"—she swallowed—"if you had talked to Miguel's mother."

I sat up, the room circling around me. "Mom!"

"Baby, lie down. I won't tell you if you don't promise to stay put."

"Mom," I wailed. But I could tell she meant it. "All right. I promise."

"Miguel is in the hospital. He'll be all right, but right now he's pretty bad."

"The flu?"

"No." She shook her head and went back to massaging my knee, as if that could take the pain from my heart. "When we dropped him off Friday night, his father—"

"He hit him."

Mom shook her head. "Worse than that. He tried to defend himself, but Jackson said he used something—lumber or something. His mother called the police, and that's when his dad went crazy. He went after her, too."

I sobbed, and Mom rocked me, her words like a blanket of horror smothering my thoughts.

"They've kept him in the hospital because there was some internal bleeding. Aidyn—"

"I want to go see him."

"Not 'til you're better."

"He won't know why I'm not there!"

"Jackson told him. He said Miguel looks really bad. They were glad you couldn't see him yet."

"But I have to—"

"You will." I felt Mom shake as she held me. "Aidyn, his dad was drunk. And I think—I think, that could have been me and you. I could have hurt you that bad. I *have* hurt you that bad." She rocked harder, and I felt her tears in my hair.

"I hope his dad is in jail this time."

"They haven't found him yet."

"I want to see Miguel *now*." I would not let his fears come true.

"You will, baby, just as soon as you can."

Mom took me two days later. He looked worse than my nightmares. At least in my dreams, I could still see his eyes. He still had his smile. Now he wore bruises and stitches in equal glory, scabs bunching on his face like pus. One eye had swollen shut, and he couldn't seem to focus the other.

Jackson said, "Hey, buddy, I brought the girl."

Miguel raised his hand, the one not attached to tubes, an inch off the white sheet.

Mom, on my other side, touched my shoulder. "I'm going to talk to your mother, Miguel. I'll be right outside."

I nodded and stared at Miguel. His open eye seemed steadier. His free hand inched toward me. A splint strapped two fingers but I slipped my hand under his and felt the rest of his fingers curl around mine.

"Oh, Miguel." Fear and pity choked me with equal intensity.

"I still say you should've done this before Halloween," Jackson teased. "You'd have made a great ghoul."

Miguel grunted, a cross between a laugh and a

croak.

"I'm gonna wait outside, too." Jackson pulled the heavy door shut behind him, and Miguel and I were alone.

"I guess you couldn't stop him." I wiped my eyes then bent to kiss his hand. I wanted so badly to feel his lips on mine, but they were covered with stitches, and it would only hurt him. "Mom said the police are looking for him."

He nodded.

"I hope they catch him. I hope they lock him up 'til he rots." Until right then I didn't know how much I hated Miguel's father. And as I sat on Miguel's hospital bed, holding the few fingers I could, I understood a little of Mom's horror that *she* could have been the monster, the same kind of monster, and I cried.

Twice after that, I visited Miguel in the hospital. Jackson and Shannon were both really good about giving me rides after school. Both times they waited for me in the hall, as if standing guard. Only when we were on the way home after the last time did Jackson explain why.

"I guess his dad's making some threats—"

"Threats?" I turned in the seat, glaring as if Jackson had been the one to make them. "Hasn't he done enough?"

"Doesn't sound like he thinks so."

"Can't they just find him? He's horrible!"

Shannon leaned over the bench seat to touch my shoulder. "We all know that, Aidyn. But that's why no one wanted to let you go there by yourself. Just in case he showed up again."

"What about when I'm not there?"

"They're watching him, I promise." Jackson

slowed to stop in front of my apartment building. "Did he tell you he's supposed to get out tomorrow?"

I nodded. "Can we do something for him? Have some sort of celebration? Lucy could do something like that, couldn't she?"

"I'll ask her," Jackson said.

And I walked up the stairs to my apartment shivering with the thought that the monster might be after me, too.

The next day the phone started ringing before I got through the door. I tossed my books on the coffee table and grabbed the receiver, hoping it would be Miguel, telling me he'd gone home.

"I'm home," he assured me, once I'd gotten over my excitement. "For now."

"You're not going somewhere now, are you? You can't, you can barely walk!"

"My mom said I could tell you now."

"What?" But a part of me broke the same way his voice did.

"We have to leave. My mom's in danger, so we have to go somewhere he can't find us."

"But you can tell me, can't you?"

"The police"—he choked on a sob—"No, Aidyn, I can't tell you. The police say it's too dangerous because the jerk could get you to tell him and then it would be useless—our hiding, I mean."

"But when are you coming back?"

"I don't know. If they find him, I guess we can come back."

"No!"

"Aidyn, please—"

"You can't leave me!"

"He hit my mom." The truth was all there in his

voice: Why he was going. Why he hadn't told me before. Why he wouldn't tell me now where they were going. Why protecting his mother meant more to him than anything.

I glanced at Mom. "Can I come see you first?"

"No, we're leaving right now." Muffled words, then he said, "Mom said she'll bring me by for a few minutes."

"Now?"

"Yeah." I heard nothing, but I felt his struggle with his tears.

Why is it that good-byes are so bleak, that your mind is already on the time when you'll be apart, already crying?

Mom and Mrs. Rosas shared tea in the kitchen while Miguel and I huddled in the living room, as though we had to hide from anyone looking in the windows. But this would be his life from now on, this hiding, this fear. The only difference would be me. I wouldn't be a part of it.

He kissed me a few times, but I could tell it hurt. He stroked my chin, my shoulder blades, and lifted my cross. "Maybe you should try to find the silver lady again. We need another miracle."

"She can't do miracles. She's just a creepy lady." My throat tightened.

"You never know." Even with the swelling down I could tell it hurt him to smile, but he tried. "Come on, Aidyn. Have a little faith."

"Faith in what? In some crazy lady who doesn't even know me? In what?"

"In God, maybe?" His smile disappeared. "I gave you that cross for a reason."

"I know. I'm sorry." I looked away. "Most of the

time, faith doesn't do me any good."

"Oh, Aidyn, I don't want to fight. I want you to think of me and remember how much—" He kissed me again. "Remember I love you," he whispered.

Before they left, his mother dug in her purse and pulled out a copy of his junior picture. She pushed it into my hand. "You keep it."

I cried hot tears and rummaged in Mom's stash of photos to find a few of myself. He limped over to me and picked up the photo of my dad and me, the same one Mom had given me.

"You don't look like him, much, except your chin. You're stubborn." He laughed.

"I look like Mom."

"You look like Aidyn. Beautiful." He held the picture out to me. "Can I keep this? I'll bring it back. I promise. Someday, I'll bring it back."

I nodded. Knowing he'd carry it with him, knowing it would bring him back to me, made it the most precious thing I owned.

I hadn't slept in Mom's bed since just after my dad died, but that night she let me crawl in with her, held me while I cried and let me tell her the plans Miguel and I made with each other but couldn't believe would ever happen.

"You'll see him again, I hope."

"You promise?"

"I can't do that. But I believe it. I believe with my whole heart that you'll see him."

I pushed her away. "What's so hard about making promises?"

"I won't make a promise I can't keep."

"Why not? You've broken plenty of them before." I knew I'd hurt her, I wanted to hurt her. Losing

Miguel wasn't Mom's fault, but she was the only person I could fight.

"You're right." Mom drew me back to her side. "And that's why I made the decision that I won't make promises I can't keep, and I'll keep the ones I make."

I sat up, searching her face in the darkness. "Then promise you'll never drink again." If only she would, how much easier my life would be.

"I can't, baby. No matter how much we both want that to be true, I can't promise."

"Then I don't want any of your promises!"

"What do you want from me?" Mom rubbed her face. "I'm doing as much as I can."

"You've made it this far. It's been almost two months, Mom. Why not?" I sounded like a begging child.

I felt her struggle, her shaking. "I can't, Aidyn. I just can't."

"So you'll start lying to me and life will turn back into chaos."

I turned my back on her and let the silence come between us. Pride said I ought to march back to my own room; pain made me stay. After a long time, Mom whispered, "Aidyn, I can promise this. If I start drinking again, I'll tell you. I won't lie about it."

At first I shrugged. Then I turned and let her hold me again. Even Mom couldn't promise Miguel would be safe. She couldn't promise I'd see him again. She couldn't promise she wouldn't drink. But at least she could hold me while I cried.

The next day, Saturday, Elaine and Jackson showed up. Shannon tagged behind, giving Mom uneasy looks, even after Mom welcomed her.

"We're going skating," Elaine announced.

"Skating," Mom said, as if it were a foreign word. She gave Elaine a look I remembered from childhood, when Dad would come up with some crazy idea and expect Mom to be as enthusiastic as he was. Usually Dad won.

"Shannon tells me she and Aidyn used to skate together all the time."

I glanced at Shannon.

"Sorry," she mouthed, and then, louder, "We thought it would take your mind off things."

"I don't want to take my mind off Miguel."

She snorted.

"Skating?" Mom repeated.

"You know, the little boots with the wheels attached to the bottom? You roll around on them, do tricks." Elaine laughed. "That sort of thing. Let's go."

"I don't know how to skate." But Mom got her keys anyway.

"Today's the day you'll learn." Elaine gave her a brilliant smile and swept us out in front of her.

As Jackson passed me I hissed, "I don't want to go skating."

"You've got to do something besides moon about Miguel."

"I *like* mooning about him."

"I told Mom it was too soon. She's got this idea that she needs to show Beth how she likes you and thinks you're this wonderful girl. They got in a fight, you know."

I shook my head.

"Yeah, Mom told her"—he stopped—"I mean…"

"Your mom can't stand me; that's no big secret."

Shannon said, "She doesn't like me either."

"OK, so it's not a secret," Jackson said. "Anyway,

Mom wants to make it up to her."

"Are you going to take all day?" Elaine asked from beside her car.

Mom was already in the front, and the three of us climbed into the backseat.

Why hadn't Mom told me they'd fought? Elaine was her sponsor. Maybe that was why she'd missed so many meetings lately. I'd thought it was because of the flu and Miguel, but a fight with Elaine made more sense. And the way she'd refused to make promises the night before. Cold chills started in my neck and spilled down my back. Maybe Mom didn't have much to hold onto anymore either.

Elaine started the engine then slapped her hands on the wheel. "We need to talk this out."

I sank down in the seat. Great. We were imprisoned. I couldn't get away without making a scene.

"You're getting to be very good at accepting responsibility for your actions, Beth. But you haven't said one word about the way you yelled at me."

"You're right. I haven't." Mom kept her voice light, though I heard the anger. "I yelled at you. I was mad. I think I still am."

Elaine nodded. "And I now need to accept responsibility for my own bad behavior. Sobriety does not make a person perfect." She twisted in the seat, her cheeks flaming. "I admit I disliked Aidyn before I ever met her—"

"Mom, she's sitting right here," Jackson said in an agonized tone.

"I realize that, son. Aidyn, the truth is, I blamed you for making things so hard for your mother. You weren't supportive, and I wanted Beth to have the support she needed."

I pinched my lips together, certain that everyone in the world saw what a horrible person I was and had judged me unacceptable.

"I was wrong." Elaine's voice strained on the words. "I realize I had it so easy during my early recovery. I had my sons, my husband, and they all backed me up. They wanted the best for me. I only wanted the best for you, Beth, and I was angry that Aidyn didn't seem to care."

Mom held up a hand. "Elaine—"

Elaine raised her voice. "I was jealous for you. I wanted so badly for you to make it, and I resented Aidyn because I thought she would make you fail."

Again, Mom tried to give Elaine her opinion. "Aidyn doesn't have that power."

"I know that." Elaine relaxed slightly and reached for the gear shift. "One of the first lessons we learn, but I forgot it in my enthusiasm to help you." She turned to meet my eyes. "Aidyn, I apologize for resenting you. Your mother's recovery is not up to you."

Tortured by raw emotion, I nodded and slid my eyes to meet Mom's.

"Now, Aidyn, if you want to help your mom, you'll go to the Alateen meetings everyone keeps bugging you about. Nobody's trying to get on your case."

I stared at my hands, thinking that "bugging" was a mild word to describe how everyone nagged me.

"I'm done," Elaine announced. She pulled away from the curb. "I've made all of you uncomfortable, I'm sure, and to make it up to you all, the skating trip is my treat."

"I don't skate." But no one paid attention to Mom.

She meant what she said, but I didn't realize how serious she was until we got inside the rink. Her face went pale when Jackson insisted on fitting her with a pair of roller blades. "I don't need them," she said, though not loud enough to convince anyone but me.

Jackson handed her the skates. "Come on, Mrs. Pierce. Show your style."

Mom stared at him, turned to me. "He's not making sense. I don't know how to skate. I don't even know how to put them on." She handed them to Elaine and walked away, but Elaine followed her. I found a bench to sit on while I changed out of my shoes. By the time I stood up, I could see Elaine had bullied Mom into lacing up a pair. Elaine grabbed her hands and pulled her up, then let go. Mom promptly went down.

I pulled her up and tried to stop laughing.

"I'm too old to start this," Mom yelled.

Jackson got on one side and Elaine got on the other, and they dragged her to the side of the rink, but that was as far as they got. Just like a horse rearing at the edge of a ditch, Mom threw her hands out to brace herself on the barrier.

"I'm not going out there."

Jackson grabbed her arm, playfully. Mom jerked away, not at all playfully, and glared at him. "I don't skate."

"It's OK, Beth," Elaine yelled. "If you're not comfortable with it, you don't have to do it."

Jackson lifted his hands in a give-up gesture before he and Shannon swooped out. I could tell they'd practiced.

"OK." Mom relaxed. She rolled one foot forward, then the other and grimaced.

"You going?" she asked me.

I shrugged. Elaine motioned me out on the rink and that was enough to make me want to plant myself next to Mom and refuse to move.

Mom leaned toward Elaine. "Give me a drink, and I'll do it."

Elaine chuckled, though I didn't see any humor in it. I turned around to argue as Elaine said, "Feeling brave, are we?"

"Actually, no." Mom shook her head. "You want the truth? It'd take the whole bottle to get me out there."

That time I yelled, "Mom!"

"Oh, Aidyn, I'm joking." Mom waved her hand as though she could brush away the words. "I'm not going to start drinking because of some roller rink."

"OK." I edged closer. "I'll sit out with you."

"What, to babysit me?"

"No, to keep you company."

Her face lit up. After watching the rink for a moment, she said, "If you promise you won't let me kill myself, maybe I'll try."

"Really?"

Elaine raised her fist in victory. "Let me get warmed up, and I'll come back to spot you."

Mom grabbed my arm and pulled herself closer, nearly pulling me down at the same time. "You have to stay with me, OK, or I won't make it."

Mom had been with me all week. "I'll stick by you."

"Don't leave me, Aidyn. Promise."

"I won't. I'll be right here next to you." I meant it. I meant it for the times she got scared, or I got scared. I meant it for the times one of us needed the other to hold on to. I meant it forever, and I never thought it might be the kind of promise I should never have made.

13

Mom bounced in from work the Monday before Thanksgiving. "I got a promotion."

I didn't get it. Mom worked with plants. What could she be promoted to? Trees? But I couldn't ask. Since Miguel had left, opening my mouth to do more than yawn took too much energy. I rubbed my eyes beneath my smeared glasses and watched Mom.

Her eyes sparkled as she danced around our old living room furniture. She'd caught her hair in a French braid that morning, and now, with the dark frizzy spits of escaped curls framing her cheeks, she looked so young and so happy. I straightened a bit, digging my elbow into the broken sofa spring to lever myself. Only in the last few weeks had her face lost the alcoholic sag she'd worn for so long. Now she looked like the mother I remembered from back when Daddy was still alive.

"I finally get to do what I've always wanted. I've been trying to prove to Toni that I could do it. She told me today that she'd always known I could, too, that I'd be really good at it, but I couldn't handle it when I was drinking." She laughed. "God bless sobriety! It means a raise, Aidyn. A big raise and commissions."

"What kind of promotion?" I scooted forward so the lumpy couch wouldn't lure me back into closing my eyes.

"I am now Toni's official landscape consultant."

She grinned. "This means I get to advise people who need help with their gardens or yards. It might be as simple as finding the right plants for the kind of sun exposure they get, or as big as plotting out a whole yard." She bounced on her toes. "And if we have more money, maybe we can get some new furniture, fix up this place. You'd like that, wouldn't you? Some new things in your room?"

"I guess." I didn't want to hurt Mom or squash her enthusiasm. I couldn't remember the last time she'd been so excited about anything. But everything she'd used to tempt me back into caring for life seemed flat, colorless, and empty. Anything without Miguel looked lifeless.

Mom danced a bag of frozen peas from the freezer to the stove. "The best thing is, I've already got a big job lined up. Someone who just moved here is coming in tomorrow to consult with me about landscaping his whole property. I can't wait, but I'm a little scared, too." She glanced at me.

"It sounds really good, Mom."

She came to kneel in front of me, her hand on my cheek. "Baby, it won't always hurt this much. I know I never taught you any decent ways to deal with losing someone you love, and all I can say is, you have hope. He's—" She stopped, her face tortured.

"He's still alive," I finished for her.

She nodded and stood. "Do you think you can help with dinner?"

I shrugged, but I followed her to the kitchen and set the table. As we ate, she asked, "Do you mind my going on and on about this? I don't want to make you feel worse, but I'd like to think I can help take your mind off Miguel, at least for a while."

"It's OK," Really, it was. While most of me cried silently for him, a small part of me rejoiced for her. Finally her world was going good, and I wouldn't let myself resent it.

After she sang her way through a sink full of dishes, she called Elaine to tell her the good news. Even on the phone she couldn't sit still but danced around the room. I heard her say, "Thanks, I'm proud of me, too," while she bounced on her toes. She sounded like a little kid, and I found myself smiling for a few seconds until I realized *I* hadn't told her I was proud of her. Should I? But I couldn't decide if it would be true or not.

While she talked I sneaked to my room. My bed was a mass of cold, tangled sheets, the blanket a twisted snake reaching for the floor. I lay across it on my stomach and reached for the tiny pile of letters I kept beside the pillow, letters I'd written to Miguel. I had no idea where he was, no idea how I could ever send anything to him. But I couldn't stop writing them. When I held them against my heart, I felt closer to him, closer to our love. Because he loved me, and I'd never told him I loved him. Not out loud. I told him over and over in the letters he never got to read.

After a while I wiped my eyes and got a new sheet of paper. I told Miguel how much I missed him and about Mom's promotion and her excitement. I told Miguel I needed him, and how kind Jackson and Shannon and Lucy, in fact, nearly everyone in the youth group, had been. I begged him to come home.

And then I crumpled the letter and threw it in the trash, because what good was it? Even if somehow I could get it to him, he couldn't do what I asked, could he? He couldn't put his mother or himself in danger, just because I wanted him. Still, after a few minutes I rescued it. I smoothed it out, folded it, and slipped it into an envelope. It held my heart, and I was not going to throw my heart away. And these letters were my only connection with Miguel now. Writing to him kept him close. No matter how pathetic I felt I had to keep them.

I stroked my cross. I hadn't taken it off again, even for the shower. *Please, keep him safe. Bring him back soon. I need him. You know how much I need him.*

The next day Shannon took me aside during our lunch break. "Have you heard anything?"

I shook my head. Mom had made a lunch for me and had made sure I tucked it in my backpack before I left for school. But I didn't know what was in it and didn't care. I ate when I felt so dizzy I thought I'd fall over but not until then. Eating was just something that kept Mom from taking me to the doctor.

"Aidyn, everyone's so worried."

"He'll come back when they catch his dad." I hoped. But how would they even know? Did *someone* know where they were? Why wasn't that someone me?

"Not so much about him. I mean, we are, but we're more worried about you."

I shrugged.

"You're really depressed, Aidyn. I think you should go talk to somebody. Jackson goes to the Alateen meetings, and we thought if you went—"

"This doesn't have anything to do with Mom's drinking!"

"But it would be someone to talk to. Or go see Lucy. She really does care."

I shook my head. "I want Miguel."

"I know but—"

A Fistful of God

I stood up and threw my full brown sack in the trash. "It's nice everybody's so worried, but there's nothing anyone can do." I walked away then turned back. "Why didn't anybody care all those years when I was depressed because of Mom? I didn't act much different then, did I? But no one noticed."

"People noticed, Aidyn. You just...you never let anyone get close. And we didn't know how bad things were. I guess that's just—I'm not making excuses. That's just the way it was."

And Miguel was gone. He might never come back, and that was just the way it was, too. The way it was stunk.

That night Mom didn't say one word about her new job. Only when I'd watched her pace the apartment for nearly an hour did I notice her agitation. She hadn't acted like this since the week after she'd quit drinking, and panic filled my stomach. Did she know something about Miguel? Or had something gone wrong at work?

"Mom, didn't you start that job today?"

She nodded.

"Mom, you're scaring me. What's wrong?"

"Oh, baby, nothing's wrong." She finally came to sit next to me on the couch, snuggling into the hollow it had grown to hold us. "Yes, I started. I got to meet the man, but—"

"What? Is he a creep or something?"

"No! No, he's—I know him, that's all. He was—Aidyn, do you remember Daddy's best friend?"

"Yeah." I bent my head. "Doug, wasn't that his name?"

She nodded. "Doug Sharpell. He's the one I'm doing this job for."

"I remember he deserted us after Dad died."

"He didn't. His job transferred him to France. He tried to keep in touch for a long time." She looked away. "I suppose I pushed him away as much as I did everyone else. But he wanted to help us."

My mind filled with long-ago memories. I remembered playing mouse in Doug's beard and opening presents he'd bring me. I still had some of those things, I thought, things that hadn't really reminded me of him but only of a sense of him. Of him and Daddy, as though he'd left his ghost with me.

"That's kind of weird, meeting him like that."

"Not really. He knew I'd started working for Toni, and he went there to find me. Things just…sort of escalated and now—"

"Now you're working for him."

She jumped up, pacing again to the hall and back to me. "Aidyn."

"Mom, you're creeping me out." But wasn't that better than sheer misery? "Don't you want to work on his house?"

"His garden. Yes, I do, but things get complicated." She bit her lip. "Too much has changed, and I'm scared. I'm not the same person. I still haven't told him—maybe Toni has."

"Oh. You mean because you're an alcoholic?"

She nodded. "He asked me out."

I closed my eyes. Mom, dating? She'd just started being Mom again, and now this? And what about Daddy? I saw him in the hospital, Mom bending over his bed, gripping his fingers as though that could keep him with her.

"Aidyn, I'm not even sure I can do this. As soon as I tell him, he may just—I'm no prize, I know that."

A Fistful of God

I thought of the letters I'd written to Miguel. I needed him to hear how badly I hurt. I needed him to care. Mom cared, a lot of people cared, but it wasn't the same, and it didn't fill the hole Miguel had left.

Daddy's death left that kind of hole in Mom, and she'd tried filling it in the most horrible way, pouring thousands of bottles into it. And now there was Doug.

I remembered sliding into the bed beside her, how she'd hold me, and we'd both cry. I swallowed and opened my eyes. "I think you should go."

She stared at me, astounded. "You do? But—"

"I think you should tell him everything, and then if he still wants to go out with you, you should go." Where did this wisdom come from? Some wise child I'd never before heard from? And what advice would this wise child give me?

I looked up. "Are you going?"

She smiled. "I think so."

"Good."

Her face relaxed and she sat with me, rocking the way she does when she wants to comfort me.

But I couldn't make myself feel any better. I struggled through a fog of confusion while I went to classes and came home to hours of lonely misery. Shannon invited me to a hundred things with her, but I turned them all down.

Finally she said, "OK, fine, stay home and sulk! When you're ready to start living again, let me know."

But that would be when Miguel returned home, and then I wouldn't need her.

On top of my own misery, I felt something else hanging over my head, something huge and black and so far, nameless. I tried to tell Mom, and we talked for a long time about it. She thought sure it had something to do with Doug. He and Mom had scheduled their first date for the Friday after Thanksgiving. Mom was nearly in a frenzy, trying to deal with her excitement and my depression at the same time.

"That's not it, Mom, I swear. I want to be happy for you."

"Is it Miguel? Are you afraid he's in trouble?"

I shook my head. Where my heart touched on Miguel was only emptiness. This thing threatened my life.

"You're scaring me, too. Creeping me out." I could tell she wanted to make me laugh.

"No. Mom, will you just stay here with me tonight? Can you stay home from your meeting this once?"

"Of course, baby. I can go tomorrow. Anyway, I brought some projects home from work. We can work on those."

"We? I don't do so good with plants," I told her. But she dragged me to the table anyway and dumped out bag after bag of surprises. Miniature pumpkins, shining gourds, sprays of oak and ash, pussy willows, eucalyptus already crumbling at the edges, dried berried clinging to brittle stems.

"These won't keep until next year and when I was packing them up I thought of how we used to make things together. Wreaths, that sort of thing. Do you want to call Shannon?"

"No, that's OK. She's probably out with Jackson, anyway." And still mad at me.

As we worked, we talked again of what I'd begun to think of as "my" obsession.

"Mom," I finally said. "I'm not getting any closer to figuring it out and talking about it is making me shake. Can we change the subject?"

I thought sure she'd bring up Doug, but instead she talked about the gifts we were making and who we'd give them to. "I promised Toni a wreath and a basket, and of course there's Elaine and the Donaldsons."

"And Doug?" I teased.

"If I see him before Thanksgiving, sure." But her cheeks stained pink, and I knew she hoped she would. "And we'll take one with us when we go to your grandmother's for—"

"No!" I grabbed Mom's arm. "We can't go. *That's* what's been bothering me."

Mom frowned. "Your grandmother? You haven't seen her since July. It's only fair—"

"Not to you."

She shook her head. "I know what you're thinking. They always have plenty of booze, and I shouldn't be anywhere near it, but I can handle it. Trust me, OK? I have to learn to live in a world that includes something I crave and can't ever touch. Other people have done it, and so can I."

"Mom, please, can't we stay home for the day? I don't care if we have tuna sandwiches, anything but going to Grandma's—" I should have known, I should have remembered sooner. What was wrong with me?

"It's a tradition," Mom said.

"Why don't we start a new tradition, just you and me? And Doug! Mom, we could invite Doug."

"He's going to his sister's up north. Baby, I don't see what you're worried about. I'll be fine."

"I don't want to go. Mom, please."

"I don't understand. Why not? They're Daddy's family. They have a right to see you. And we have a responsibility to them, too."

"I don't care."

"Aidyn, I promise, I'll be fine. Come on. Let's deliver our gifts and then I'll treat us to dinner, OK?"

But the black dread hovered over me. As we got home again with our bags of fast food, the phone rang. Mom grabbed it, and I saw by her smile she thought it might be Doug. Instead, she frowned. "Roy?" A pause, then, "Oh, no. No! Why?"

I moved closer and leaned against her. She crossed her free arm, listening, whimpering. Who was it, and what was wrong? Doug? Miguel? When she hung up she closed her eyes and swayed where she was. I led her to the couch and took off her coat. She pulled her hat across her face to her lap and stared at it, limp in her hands. "That was Joyce's husband."

I relaxed. Joyce, Mom's drinking buddy. She hadn't mentioned her in weeks, and whatever Roy told Mom couldn't matter.

"She's dead." Mom covered her face with her hands and shook, but when she straightened, I saw no tears. "Her funeral was Monday, and he just now thought to tell me." Her words slurred.

"Mom." I sat next to her and tried to get her to stop rocking. "I'm sorry." Just because I hated Joyce, hated what Mom was like around her, didn't mean Mom wouldn't miss her.

"She took a bottle of pain killers and mixed it with whiskey." Mom finally focused on me. "She stopped talking to me. She said I was trying to reform her. If I'd known I could have—I've taken her to the hospital to get her stomach pumped before."

I hadn't known that. So much of Mom's life since Daddy died I didn't know, but it was stuff I ought to

A Fistful of God

know. I'd been living with her, after all.

"I should have called her," Mom said. "If only—"

"You couldn't have stopped her. She did it before, didn't she?"

"And I saved her then."

No matter what I said, I couldn't get Mom to admit Joyce's death hadn't been her fault.

By the next morning some of Mom's shock had worn off. Her eyes were puffy from crying and she still wore the haunted fear in her eyes. But she packed up the dessert she'd made to share with Daddy's family and drove there with steady hands.

"Mom, we really don't have to go," I told her. That phone call had fueled my dark cloud of fear. "Nobody would blame you—"

"I can't keep running away. I'll be fine."

As soon as we walked in the door Grandma started gushing. "I called everyone else," she whispered, but so loud that the guys crowded in front of the televised football game heard. "We all want to help poor Beth *so much*. So everyone agreed we'd give up our little dinner drinks, just for today."

"That wasn't necessary." Mom's lips pinched, and I wondered if Grandma could tell how angry Mom was.

But some of my dread abated. Without temptation, Mom would be safe. I walked into the hallway behind her, trying to catch sight of her face. Was she mad because Grandma was so condescending, or because she'd removed the booze from easy access? With the mood Mom had been in all day, it could have been either. I found myself twisting my hat until Mom took it and hung it up over my coat.

"You might have been right," she said.

"We could go home," I whispered.

She shook her head then led me into the kitchen where two of my aunts and a cousin were cooking.

All the adults acted glad to see us and exclaimed over how much I'd grown and how pretty I'd gotten. I rolled my eyes whenever I heard that. Everyone but Grandma carefully avoided any mention of Mom's sobriety. I got the idea they were embarrassed. But what was worse, admitting she was an alcoholic and trying to quit, or actively *being* that alcoholic?

I wandered out of the kitchen for a while. My cousins had dubbed Grandma's house "the shrine", and it was—a shrine to my father. His picture hung in every room, and this year she'd added a table with candles and fresh flowers arranged on it, along with cards he'd drawn in grade school. Back in the kitchen, I listened as Grandma's voice grew louder and more slurred. I tried to catch Mom's eye, but she spent most of her time staring at her hands or the potatoes she was peeling.

So much for Grandma's no-little-drinks rule. She must have had bottles stashed in every room. She staggered out of the kitchen so often I thought she'd wear a hole through the old linoleum. I leaned on the door between the dining room and the kitchen, the roar of the game like a cushion behind me, the disorder in the kitchen in front of me. I didn't know what to expect, but I wanted to be close to Mom. I wanted to be able to pull her to safety if I had to. When Grandma dropped a bowl of creamed peas on the floor, the kitchen exploded.

Aunt Lena, Dad's sister, started. "Crap, Mother, I thought we weren't supposed to be drinking here." She glared at Mom.

"We're no...we're not. Sshh!" Grandma tried to cover her mouth with her finger, missed, hit her ear, and winked.

"Isn't it nice to know you're not the only drunk in the family?" Aunt Lena hissed at Mom. I wanted to spit on her.

"She's your mother," Mom said. "Why don't you do something for her?"

"What?" Lena barreled up and got in Mom's face. "What do you suggest? Some hospital where she can dry out? What?"

"How about some compassion?" Mom looked around, met every eye that was on her. "This is a rough day."

"Made even rougher by our enforced sobriety."

The volume of the TV went down and one of my uncles said, "Sshh." I took a step toward Mom.

Once started, Aunt Lena couldn't seem to stop. "I don't blame Mother for drinking, not at all. I just wish you'd have had the courtesy to let the rest of us drown our sorrows, too."

Mom's face went blank. She put her hands behind her as though feeling for the edge of a precipice. I grabbed her and dragged her to the door, shoved her into her coat, and slapped her hat on her head. And then I turned and called my aunt a name that insured no one would mind that I never came back to that house again.

"We shouldn't have come," I told Mom. "But it's OK. We're going now."

"Don't start, please," Mom whispered as she fumbled for her keys.

"I didn't mean to." I held her purse while she unlocked the car door. Behind us, the noise of the game shut off as if someone had slammed the door. I looked back.

"They don't even care." I stomped around and got in the passenger side. "All they care about is themselves, not us. I don't want to be a part of that kind of family."

"Aidyn, please." Mom started the engine.

"We shouldn't have gone."

"You said that. Can you let it go now?"

"Why? They're all jerks. Grandma's a drunk and Aunt Lena's a—"

"Aidyn!" Her hands clenched the wheel, and I stared at her. Behind her burning eyes her face went white.

"And right now, my mom wants to get just as plastered as Grandma."

"Don't start with me!"

"Then stop wishing you had a bottle of booze!"

"You don't know what I want!"

I cowered in the corner, terrified of both of us. "What, then?"

"I want you to leave me alone."

Of course she did. I wasn't helping her at all, was I? I fumbled with my hat, wishing it could muffle my sobs. When she stopped for a light I jerked the door open and tumbled out.

"Aidyn!"

I slammed the door. "You got what you wanted, OK? I'm gonna leave you alone." I headed back the way we'd come, so she couldn't follow me. If she went around the block and stopped for me, I thought, I'd get in. I'd apologize.

She didn't. I gave her enough time to circle the block twice, then gave up waiting and turned for home. I stayed on the streets she always drove to give her the chance to find me if she wanted.

She didn't. I rubbed the chill on my arms and stamped my feet. I hadn't noticed the cold before. I trudged home, calling myself worse names than I'd called Aunt Lena. How could I be so stupid? Why couldn't I have given Mom a break? Why hadn't she come back for me?

As soon as I walked through the apartment door, I knew why.

I smelled the scotch.

14

Mom slumped on the couch, her coat half on, as though she couldn't bear to waste time to shrug it off. Her face wore the worst look I had ever seen, as though she knew she'd done something wrong, something horrible. She *knew* and didn't care. The bottle sat on the table in front of her, half empty. She'd guzzled it that fast.

She looked up at me, swaying even while she sat, and raised her glass to me. Booze sloshed over her hand. "Oops." She licked it off, spilling still more that she didn't notice.

I backed away. "No. No. I *hate* you." Tears clogged my throat.

Mom flinched.

"You couldn't leave it alone, could you? Grandma was having so much fun." The smell and my anger ganged up on me, and I gagged.

"She's pathetic." Mom sipped reverently. "That's good."

"You're worse than she is."

"You're right." She laughed, set the glass on the table, and tried to stand. She fell back twice and finally managed to get to her feet.

This couldn't be happening. This could not be my mom, the mom I'd finally started to trust again. This couldn't be!

"You're nothing but a drunk."

Mom ignored that. "I should've gone ba-back for you. I knew that. You knew tha-that. I was just stupid." Her face crumpled. "Stupid, stupid, stupid."

I slapped her face. I didn't feel it at all, but she did.

She staggered away from me, knocking into the glass and sending a golden arch to stain the carpet.

"You're nothing but a drunk!"

Mom straightened and stared at me, tears pouring down her face. I watched the mark of my hand flame red on her skin. After a minute, Mom leaned past me to collar the neck of the bottle and carried it to the kitchen. As I stooped to pick up the glass she'd sidestepped I heard something clink. Another glass? She didn't need it. She was drunk enough. I ran toward the kitchen, wanting to choke her, her addiction, her demons, anything.

Mom held the bottle upended over the sink and poured the rest down the drain. The bottle slipped, and she jerked. Shattered glass rained into the sink. She tried to grab it, gasped, and in seconds her blood mixed with the booze.

She looked at me. "You're right, baby, I'm a dru-drunk." She turned her hands, cupping blood and scotch and broken glass. "I'll always be a drunk. Ca— can't fix that now. But may—maybe I can be more'n that, you think?"

But I didn't *want* my mother to be a drunk.

She moved toward me and scarlet ribbons streamed across the tiles and my stomach heaved.

"I make m'stakes, Aidyn. I always do. But I don't have to make—make the same ones, do I? Do I?" She swayed, her face white. "I don'—don' want—wanna drink anymore."

I grabbed her wrist and twisted her hands so she'd

drop the shards but her fingers wrapped tighter and still more blood oozed. "Let it go, Mom. Drop it."

"Yeah. Let it go." She sighed and the last few bits of glass fell. She blinked at her hands and her eyes widened. She fell against me, and I had to push her against the counter so she'd stay put.

I held her hands under the running water. She let me wash the blood off, swaying with her eyes closed, her lashes wet on her pale face.

"Mom, I have to make sure the glass is out of all the cuts."

She nodded. I thought she must not have understood what I meant.

"It's gonna hurt, Mom, but you have to stand still."

"I will." She leaned a little closer and propped her elbows next to the sink. I prodded her hands and her blood washed over my fingers. She moaned once then turned to watch my face as I worked. Neither of us spoke. Every time her blood gushed from a cut, the world paled and I shook harder. After I'd finished I folded a clean dishtowel around her hands and tucked the ends under to hold it in place.

"Aidyn—"

"I don't want to talk to you." I turned her and pushed her toward the living room.

"I'm sorry."

"No, you're not."

"I didn't promise you I wouldn't drink." She stumbled, and I grabbed her elbow, jerking her up. I didn't know how she could have had time, but she'd probably had way more than just that half bottle. That wouldn't have made her so drunk so fast, would it? Used to be I could tell, but I'd let myself forget.

"You were just waiting for a good excuse." I spun her in front of the couch and shoved her down. Since I'd wrapped her hands together she couldn't catch herself and sprawled across the cushions.

She hitched up on one elbow, trying to yank her hands apart. "There is no good excuse."

"Yeah, well, you don't need one, do you? All you need is a bottle."

"Baby, I'm sorry—"

I swore.

Mom winced. "Aidyn, please, don't give up on me."

I left her and bolted for my room. After I dumped the books and pens from my backpack, I stuffed in some underwear, another pair of jeans and an extra sweater. I dug in a drawer and pulled out my babysitting money.

I'd been saving to buy Mom a cross. Half an hour ago I still thought she deserved it, believed she'd understand all it would mean when she unwrapped it. That I was proud of her. That I appreciated all the stuff she'd done for me. That I wasn't mad anymore.

Half an hour ago, I hadn't seen through her lies.

My vision blurred, and I collapsed on the bed. Mom called me. I jerked up then made myself sit down again. I was done with taking care of her.

The last two months had been so perfect. *Mom* had been perfect. She'd loved me. Why had she stopped? Why had I let her leave me on the street when I knew how crazy Grandma made her? No. I'd been the one to leave her. Why? Why had I ruined things? Why had *she*? And now everything was horrible. Nothing would ever be good again.

I shoved the money in my backpack and threw in

a few pairs of socks.

In the kitchen I added a bottle of water and a couple of packets of cheese crackers. I went through the living room and Mom asked, "Where are you going?"

She sounded scared. She'd pulled the towels loose, though not off, and tried to push herself off the couch. She couldn't.

I shrugged. "Out."

"Out where?" She jerked her arms and the towel unwound completely. The blood had already browned on the edges, though I could see fresh, jagged spurts on her hands. She leaned on the couch to help herself up and gasped with pain. "Aidyn, please, don't leave me."

"What do you care?" I snatched up the towel and wrapped her hands again, pulling tighter than I needed to. "You've got your booze. You don't need me."

"No, it's gone. I only got the one bottle." She raised her eyes to mine. "I swore I'd only drink one bottle."

"You can't. You know that." I turned away.

"I know. Aidyn, please—"

"Will you stop?" I pulled on my jacket and picked up my backpack.

"Aidyn? I don't want to drink anymore."

"That's nice." I slid the straps over my shoulders. "Don't take the towel off. You'll bleed to death."

I slammed the door and heard her again, not understanding her words, but her voice tore at my heart. Still, I went on through the empty courtyard and out to the street.

I wanted Miguel. He'd understand. With a deep breath, I wiped the tears off my face and started to walk. Where could I go? On Thanksgiving, who would want me to show up on their doorstep, all packed up and ready to move in?

Shannon? No. Shannon wouldn't understand. She still thought Mom was wonderful—a scary drunk, but wonderful any other time. She thought my whole life could be solved with a pep talk. She'd give me one and convince her mom to give me a ride home. I shuddered. I did not want to face Shannon's mother.

If I went to Jackson's, I'd have to face Elaine. She'd blame me. Again. I stopped for a light and wanted to collapse right there. Across the street, I saw people inside a convenience store, probably the one where Mom bought that bottle.

She poured it out, a tiny voice said, but I told it to shut up. So what if she poured it out? So what? Mom was drunk, and I didn't care if the world ended right there or not. Better if it did.

I stared into the lighted window and *hated* my mother. Her drunkenness had always been a living thing, panting its sodden breath down my back, strangling me in booze-scent. I hated *it*, wanted to crush its power with my anger. But how could I destroy something that didn't care what it hurt?

I stopped to dig in my pocket and fished out enough money for a phone call, jammed it into the pay phone and, before I could change my mind, punched in the numbers. Jackson answered.

"Hey, Jackson, it's me."

"Aidyn? What's wrong?"

"Nothing." Great, I was as big a liar as Mom. Worse. "I need to talk to your mom."

"She's kinda busy with the turkey. You want me to tell her to call you back?"

"No. Please, Jackson. It'll only take a second."

"Wait a minute. Why do *you* want to talk to Mom? Something's wrong."

I heard a scuffle, then Elaine's strong voice. "Aidyn, what's going on?"

"It's my mom." I swallowed. Could I even say this? I never had, not like this, even though a thousand times in my head I'd played it out—how I would ask for help, if ever I found someone who'd care. "She started drinking again."

"Oh, Aidyn, I'm sorry."

"That's not it. She got cut. She's bleeding. A lot. I think maybe she needs to go to the hospital."

"I'll be right there, but honey, you need to call the emergency number."

"No. I'm not home, OK? Can you do it? I don't have any more change."

Then, before she could order me to do something I didn't want to, I hung up and started to run.

15

The farther I ran from home, the more I wondered where I'd end up. I knew better than to think life for a runaway was wonderful or easy or even healthy. I could end up dead if I wasn't careful, or even if I was. But right then, if I had to choose between dead and Mom…

Well, I just might not pick Mom.

The only person who'd understand was Miguel. Chills seeped under my coat and snaked down my neck. Where was he? How could I find him? I squinted into the sunset. Clouds billowed up behind the mountains, promising rain. I had to find shelter.

I would not go back home. I thought of watching Mom weave around the apartment with the glass she couldn't put down. I thought of listening to her heave over the toilet, or into the sink, or wherever she happened to be. I thought of the smell of vomit and liquor-laced sweat. I thought of trying to reason with someone who'd drunk her reason away.

No. I wouldn't go back to that. I wouldn't give in to her again or let her push me around with her bottle.

I needed Miguel. And Miguel might—just might—be in Pasadena. I headed west toward the sun. Pasadena was about ten miles away. It could be ten thousand, though, and I'd walk until I found him. But I'd probably get there in a few hours. If I walked fast and didn't stop and didn't get lost. I'd have to stay on the main streets to keep from getting lost.

Walking warmed me, too much. Sweat soaked my sweater and when I moved, the cloth under my armpits chafed. I kept walking. I passed the high school and more houses. And the street fair, empty now, and eerie. I reached up and clutched my cross. Where had the silver lady gone? The same place Miguel and his mother had? But she wasn't running away from her monsters, was she? Heck, she even thought I was good. I wasn't good. I was selfish and stupid and stubborn, and I would not go back home.

Don't think about Mom.

I imagined Miguel's delight when I found him, how he'd fold me in his arms and kiss me before he'd take me to see his mother. Mrs. Rosas would cry, but she wouldn't ask any questions. Instead, she'd give me clean clothes and let me take a long bath and then I'd share their Thanksgiving dinner. We'd all drink ginger ale, and after that Miguel would hold me, and nothing would hurt either of us ever again.

Streetlights tricked me into seeing sidewalk cracks that weren't really there, and I stumbled over nothing. The sun had given barely any warmth, but once it went down I started to shake. I needed to find a place to rest. Not stop. I wouldn't stop until I found Miguel.

Beyond the race track. Beyond the hospital. Was Mom there right now? I looked up at the windows and imagined her holding her hands out for the doctor to stitch.

No! *Don't think about Mom.*

I saw the mall and decided I'd rest there, then angle north for a while and get past the freeway. Pasadena was only a few miles farther.

Even though the mall was closed, cars were

scattered in the parking lot. Why? I shook harder and realized I needed to walk farther to find a safe place. I didn't want to go home, but I didn't want to end up raped or murdered, either. I wanted to end up with Miguel and my everlasting happy ending.

That made me smile for half a block at least, and then I realized I could barely put down my left foot. I must have walked a blister into my heel. I had to stop, but not in the open.

Across the street I saw the huge swath of the Arboretum, a haven. Mom used to take me there on Tuesdays, when admission was free, and let me throw corn to the peacocks.

Don't think of Mom.

I stumbled across the empty parking lot and under the trees to the main gate. Just before the gate, a path snaked to the gift shop, taking a dip and a turn. No one could see it, and I'd be sheltered. All I knew was that I couldn't go any farther that night.

Without the heat of walking I shook harder than ever. I opened my backpack and took out every piece of clothing I could add to what I was already wearing, but it was like adding cheesecloth. Nothing helped. I'd have to get up soon. I'd have to walk to keep warm. My feet hurt, but I was afraid to take my shoes off to see the damage. My muscles twitched and stung. When I tried to shift to a more comfortable position I could barely move. I was such a wimp. A little bit of walking, a little bit of cold, and I was ready to surrender.

My stomach rumbled. I dug the crackers out of my backpack and swallowed almost without chewing. I hadn't eaten since breakfast. I drank the water in one long gulp and the mental picture of me, my head back as I drained the last drops, reminded me of Mom and her bottle.

Don't think about Mom.

I felt better. The food warmed me just enough to think I could make it through the night without freezing to death. I'd find Miguel in the morning.

I curled up and tried to get my coat and the extra sweater to cover my legs and head at the same time. The concrete under me shot needles of cold through me. I wrapped myself around my backpack, trying to keep as much of myself as possible off the ground. I needed Miguel. I needed his warmth.

I played my imaginary movie in my mind again, paused on the look in Miguel's eyes when he saw me, savored the way he'd treasure me and take care of me. I needed someone to take care of me, and I didn't have anybody. I couldn't count on anybody but Miguel, and he didn't know I needed him yet.

Yes, he did. But he knew his mother needed him more.

The aftertaste of fake cheese filled my mouth, and I wondered what Mom had eaten. Probably nothing. She'd started a binge and that meant no food, just the booze, until she passed out. Her Thanksgiving feast had been a bottle.

No. Don't think about Mom.

Half asleep, I jerked. Wine. I smelled wine. I sat up but only the scents from the few night plants still growing there surrounded me. It had been a dream. That was all, a nightmare starring Mom's favorite thing in the world.

Don't think about Mom.

I wrapped my fingers around my cross, my mouth trembling as I accused God. "Why did You let her start drinking again? Everything was going so good, and I prayed. You know I prayed. You must have heard me! You're just like everyone else. You make promises and then You let people down."

He didn't give me any more answers than usual, and I figured I might as well stop asking.

When I woke I had to pee so badly I nearly cried, and I ended up squatting in a bush and wetting my jeans. After I struggled out of them and into the dry ones, I stuffed the nasty ones behind a bush. If someone found them—well, they'd never know they were mine, would they? They'd probably imagine a couple of kids out screwing around, doing stupid stuff and leaving the evidence behind. As I stood up, daylight showed my hiding place hadn't been as protected as I'd imagined. It didn't matter. I was safe, and I wouldn't be there the next nightfall.

I headed north under the freeway, along the main street lined with houses and hedges. It took me hours to find a restaurant cheap enough to suit me. I bought a breakfast burrito because it reminded me of Miguel. I sat at a small table and held my backpack under it. Hunkered down, so no one could see, I counted my money.

Enough for two crosses for Mom. Forget her. It would feed me for a week at least, long enough to find Miguel. After that, I wouldn't need money. I'd be in paradise.

After a visit to the restaurant's real, bush-less bathroom, I marched out to the street. Now I could find Miguel. I had all day, didn't I?

I stood on the sidewalk, tears pouring down my face, fogging my glasses. In the daylight, in this real, huge town, I knew I'd never find Miguel, even if I was right and he was there. He and his mother wanted to hide; they wouldn't wait out in the open for me. But I needed him. Who would hold me? Who would tell me it wasn't my fault?

I'd come this far, and I had no choice but to go on. I'd wander around Pasadena for a few days. Maybe I'd see Miguel anyway. Maybe he'd see me. Maybe he'd be looking out the window as I passed by, and he'd run out and grab me in one of his crushing hugs. Then he'd take me inside to his mother, to where we would all be safe.

I went to the fast food places with the cheapest food, just for the chance to sit in their warmth and use their bathrooms. Each time it took longer for the needles to prickle out of my feet, and longer still to make myself get up again. I must have formed a thousand blisters and burst them all, but I wouldn't take off my shoes to look.

When I stopped for dinner, a small boy edged up to me, offering me a smile. Just as I grinned at him, his mother jerked him out of my view. I gaped at her. I'm a babysitter, I wanted to say, and a good one! Andy and Lucas love me, and they know I'd never hurt them. I would never hurt any kid.

Who'd believe me? I needed a shower and a comb, or at least a washcloth for my face.

I needed Miguel.

If he was hiding, where would he go? Not any place his father might drive by and catch sight of him. He'd be tucked away in some deep corner, someplace along with a thousand other kids who needed to hide from their monsters.

Yeah, I needed to find him because I had a monster, too.

I forced myself outside and got myself thoroughly lost. If I stayed on the same street, I was bound to run into some place familiar, and figure out where I was, wasn't I? Just because I didn't want to be found didn't mean I wanted to be lost.

Wait. That was Miguel and his mom who wanted to hide, not me. Right? I couldn't remember anymore.

Was anyone looking for me? Not Mom. She wouldn't notice I'd gone. If she did, she'd be glad. Elaine? If she'd taken Mom to the hospital, she might notice I still wasn't home when they got back, but she'd probably decide I was sulking somewhere and not worry about it. She'd just plan how she'd chew me out for deserting Mom when she needed me.

Don't think about deserting Mom. Don't think about Mom at all.

The sun set by the time I came to a busy street lined with the hulking skeletons of bleachers. I stared, mystified, until I spotted an ad for Rose Parade seating. I must have found Colorado Boulevard. The city erected bleachers long before New Year's Day. Across the street, behind another bleacher, I saw the city college. Security lights spotted the buildings, and I knew where I'd spend the night.

I scouted the wide-open quad and decided against its unprotected state. Raindrops pelted my face. The campus must have plenty of hidden places where I could stay dry. I slipped my backpack from my aching shoulders and wriggled them. Maybe I had blisters there, too, to match the ones on my feet.

Only the thought of Miguel, or no thoughts at all, had carried me this far. How long could I go on looking for him? Until I ran out of money? Until the blisters got infected and I couldn't stand? Until I couldn't hope, couldn't lie to myself, couldn't seduce myself with dreams that I knew would never come true?

By the time I reached a ramp that twisted and curled on itself, providing another concrete cave, I was sobbing. Across a short corridor I saw the doors to an auto shop, and the scent of grease and tires filled the damp air. Under the ramp redolent of cat pee and garbage, I found a hollowed out cave. I wondered if some other runaway had hidden there, and what had happened to her. I wondered what would happen to me. I curled around my backpack, crying from pain inside and out and wondered if I'd give up the next day.

I don't know how long I'd slept when something slammed me awake. I screamed and something rolled on top of me, pinning me with the smell of booze and unwashed body. I gagged and tried to push it off.

"What you doing here?" the monster asked.

His voice, heavy and slurred, spurred me. I pushed him away and made it to the bottom of the ramp before he caught me.

"You're just a kid." He fell against the rail, pulling me off balance. "What you doing squatting in my place?"

"I'll leave. Just let me go."

He snorted, and his hand stroked the arm of my coat as he swore at me. "You lyin'. Gimme something to drink. Gimme your money."

"I don't have any."

He swore again and threw me against the rail, then his hand clipped my jaw and my knees collapsed. As I fell, he grabbed my arm and jerked up, and my whole back burned.

"If you're lying to me, I'll kill you." He said it so casually I knew he meant it. "You get out of my place, and I won't bother you none. Hear?"

I nodded and tried to stand. But I couldn't leave. I needed my backpack but I'd left it on the ground behind him.

"Go on," he snarled. "You oughta be peeing your pants now. Don't you have any sense?"

He staggered a bit, lurching in laughter, and stopped. "This yours?" He leaned over, swiped at my backpack, and finally snagged one of the straps. It took him a few minutes to work the zipper, and I could only watch, pain and fear rooting me. When he pulled out my roll of bills, I knew I'd lost. I'd never find Miguel now.

"What you doing with this? This is gonna buy me some good stuff. Oh, baby, you made my night, lemme tell you." He rumbled toward me, and I jumped out of his way, holding my arm so the jolts wouldn't hurt so much. "Sweetest thing in the world." He wasn't talking to me anymore.

I backed away. I should have run when he let go of me instead of wishing after my backpack. Would I die now over such a stupid mistake?

But he staggered past me, dragging my backpack with him, chortling.

I was safe again.

I wanted Miguel so bad I could taste his hugs. I could hear his voice telling me he loved me and would take care of me forever.

No. He wouldn't. He couldn't. He couldn't save me from this drunk who slept in cat pee and robbed kids. He couldn't save me from Mom's drinking, and he couldn't save me from my own mistakes.

I crumpled to the bottom of the ramp and cried. I wanted Miguel, and I couldn't have him. I wanted Mom. I wanted her—sober, drunk, passed out, never able to help me, I didn't care. I wanted her. I closed my eyes, rubbed my aching shoulder. OK, I wanted Mom, and I knew where she was.

I wiped my runny nose on my jacket sleeve and pulled myself up and out of the concrete cave. The rain washed over me, poured down my neck, and soaked my hair. I tipped my head back and let it mix with the tears and wash them away. I'd given up on Mom for the last time. From now on, I'd just wait her drinking out. I would wait forever, if I had to. If I got home. If she let me come home. If she hadn't bled to death.

Elaine would have taken care of her, wouldn't she?

I planned every inch of my life from then on as I trudged to the street. The morning mist lit the way though the sun hadn't risen yet, but enough that I could see where I was headed. As soon as I got home I'd check on Mom. I'd get rid of all the booze she'd stashed and as soon as she sneaked more in, I'd find it and pour it out, too. And as soon as she sobered up, we'd talk. It would be different this time, I swore to myself, because she'd said she didn't want to drink anymore, because—

Because why? Because I'd force her to dry up? I couldn't make her stop drinking, I knew that. I'd tried a million times in the first three years. Before I gave up on her the first time.

I took a break on a bus bench, stretching my legs and trying to stretch my shoulder and my mind. No, I couldn't make Mom do anything. I couldn't make her drink or not drink. But I could be there for her as she tried once again to quit. I just had to figure out a way to keep myself from going crazy.

That Alateen program that everyone pushed at me, the meetings they said were so great. Maybe, *maybe* I'd give one a try. At least there I wouldn't be an outsider. Everyone else would be just as screwed up as I was.

I got up and limped closer to home. Was Mom looking for me? Why would she, though? I'd walked out on her when she needed me. She'd be glad to be rid of me, especially now that she'd decided to start drinking again. Would she care that I cared, that I wanted her? Would she care that I wanted to come home?

She knew she shouldn't drink. She wanted to stop. I'd read her face when she said it. That wish was so true for her, it was her center. She'd promised me she wouldn't lie and promised she wouldn't make promises she couldn't keep. She'd poured the rest of the bottle down the sink, and she'd said she didn't want to drink anymore, and even though that wasn't a promise, it somehow seemed stronger than any promise.

Well, hadn't I made promises, too? Hadn't I said I'd stay with her as long as she needed me? Hadn't I broken it? And yet I still remembered how much I loved her when I said it.

She was the drunk, but she hadn't broken any promises this time. I had.

Maybe she knew I needed her, but how could she know I wanted her? How could she know I loved her?

I'd left her with bleeding hands and a towel to sop the blood. I didn't know why my mother had to be a drunk, or why I had to become a monster—a putrid, pus-filled, hate-filled repulsive nothing.

Oh, God, I'm sorry. Help me get home. Don't let me be too late. Please! Oh, God, I want my mom!

16

Two days of walking had shredded my feet. By late afternoon, all I could think of was home, Mom, and, how much I hurt. I couldn't stop thinking about what I'd find when I reached the apartment. And what could be, if we both could let it. And what ought to be, if things were as perfect as I'd imagined before. If Mom wanted to climb out of the muck and vomit of her drinking, who was I to stop her? But I couldn't help wondering what state Mom might be in now. If she could give in to the bottle when she was upset but sober, what would she do when she was frantic and half-drunk?

Three times I stopped to make a collect call, but I never got through. Twice, the busy signal, once, no answer. The busy signal turned into a promise for me. Me, who'd given up on promises. But if Mom was home and on the phone, at least I knew she was alive. She hadn't bled to death. I stumbled along the street, sobbing, not caring that I earned more strange looks than ever before. I clung to the sound of a busy signal.

"I'm not *just* a drunk," Mom had said. And, "I don't want to drink anymore." I clutched those words and I hung onto my cross, too, my fist tight around it, dragging the chain against my neck. *Please, God*. Please, *what*, I had no idea, but God ought to be able to figure out what I needed.

I had hours more walking before I made it home,

and my feet hurt so badly I didn't think I could do it. But I had to. I'd gotten myself this far, and I couldn't expect anyone to show up and stop me from making more of an idiot of myself. What if I made one more promise to God. Let me get home safe, and I'll—what? What *hadn't* I already promised?

Keep her sober, and I'll never yell at her again. Keep her sober, and I'll go to Mass every Sunday of my life. I'll be good, and I'll never whine about Miguel. I'll stop lying even if it's just to make her feel better. Keep her sober, and I'll go to those stupid meetings.

And now, I promised God if He would get me home, I wouldn't care if she was drunk or not. But no. I would care. I just wouldn't whine.

As I trudged along Colorado Avenue, past motels and car dealerships and shoe stores, I thought of Andy, and the way he used to grab hold of my shirt even when he slept. He wouldn't let me put him down. Maybe I needed to be like that little kid where it came to God. Maybe I needed to make sure I never let go of Him.

I refused to stop. If I did, I'd never start again. I dug my freezing hands in my coat pockets, wondering if I could come up with one more terrific bribe for God so He'd pick me up out of the stinking street and whisk me home without my having to take another step. What would Lucy say? Not about making bargains with God but about what God might want. I couldn't remember anything she'd said. Wait. I remembered the day she'd told me to keep my thankfulness.

I snorted. What a stupid thing to remember. What did I have to be thankful for? My own stupidity? The fact that alcohol was invented? Mom?

What? God wanted me to be thankful for Mom?

And what if He said yes? What if that was His side of the bargain?

So I ought to think about Mom and be thankful.

In the middle of the next block, a sports car pulled a U-turn and squealed against the curb beside me. I bolted halfway across someone's lawn before I heard him. "Aidyn!"

I spun around, hobbled back to the sidewalk and peered through the open window.

"Aidyn, it's Doug Sharpell. Do you remember me?"

Mouse-fingers playing in his beard and laughing with Daddy. Mom's face when she talked about him. I nodded.

"Mind if I give you a ride?"

I hadn't even made that bargain with God, and He'd kept His end of it.

I collapsed into the seat and watched the electric window close me away from the cold. I tasted the warmth of his heater, and I settled into the soft seat, sighing.

"I'll take you wherever you say, but I hope you let me take you home."

"Oh, home. I want to go home."

He didn't start the car right away. When I turned to see why, I caught his grin. "I'm going to call your mother. Do you want to talk to her?"

"I do, but I don't want to get out of the car."

He handed me a cell phone and leaned his elbow on the steering wheel, waiting. I punched in our number and for once, Mom answered.

"Mom?"

"Oh, Aidyn. Oh, thank You, God. You're alive. Are you all right? Where are you?"

"I'm with Doug. Mom, I'm sorry."

But at the same time Mom was saying the same thing, "I'm sorry," over and over. We were like a chorus that couldn't get its tempo down. Then she said something I couldn't catch and my heart broke again. But I'd made a promise. "Mom, listen, I'm coming home. Are you listening?"

"Yes."

"I'm coming home." I choked and couldn't go on. Finally I got out, "Mom?"

"I haven't been drinking. Not since you left, baby. OK? I promised I wouldn't lie to you, and I meant it."

"I know."

"I love you, Aidyn. Maybe I can't prove it but—"

"You don't have to. Mom, I just want to come home now, OK?"

Doug took the phone then and told Mom how long it would be before we'd get there, then snapped it off and started the engine. I closed my eyes, playing the sound of Mom's voice over the phone, steady, serious, scared, loving.

"Aidyn? Are you asleep?" I shook my head and he said, "I don't want to scare you, but your Mom's hands are pretty bad. She needed a lot of stitches."

"Did Elaine take her?"

"No, I did. She called me, and I came right over and took her to the hospital while Elaine and Jackson and a whole gang of people from your youth group went looking for you."

"Really?"

"I have never heard such fear in anyone's voice. Your mother was terrified, worrying about what you'd do."

"She was drunk." I slapped my hand over my

mouth. What gave me the right to tell him that?

"I think," Doug said slowly, "a lot of that had already worn off. Shock does that to you."

I watched him for a minute. He kept his eyes on the road though I'm sure he felt me staring. Had I already ruined things for Mom?

"Did she tell you?" I whispered.

"That she'd been drinking again? Yes."

"And that—"

He didn't fill in for me that time.

"That she's—"

Why couldn't he make it easy for me?

"That she's an alcoholic?" My stomach dropped when I whispered the word.

"She did." He sighed.

"She was afraid to tell you." I stretched, and my blistered feet pressed the insides of my shoes. They'd gotten to be so sensitive that it felt like flames licking the sores. I swallowed and tried to ignore the pain. "She wouldn't have lied to you, though."

Doug laughed. He stopped for a light and turned to me, his hand stroking his beard. "She certainly didn't lie. She walloped me with the details. I got the idea she was trying to scare me off."

"But she likes you."

He turned forward again. "I'm glad. I like her, too, but I can see she's very unsure of herself. That would be natural, though."

"Why?"

He glanced at me. "Why do you think she started drinking so heavily in the first place?"

I didn't answer. The car's heat made me sweat and reminded me of how long it had been since I'd showered. I wondered if he could smell my stink. I wondered if I sickened him. But then, Mom hadn't.

"Aidyn, listen, we've got a lot to work through. Well, of course, you and Beth have done a lot, but you've got a lot more to do." I expected him to give me another mini-commercial for Alateen. "I knew your mom had a bit of a drinking problem. I've tried to keep in touch, you know, and it was pretty obvious. I wish—hindsight speaking now—I wish I'd come back a long time ago, but I don't know if I could have changed things for her. Or for you."

So we all felt guilty. I sat up. "For me?"

"Being the child of an alcoholic isn't easy."

He wasn't kidding. I watched the familiar streets pass. Being Mom's daughter wasn't going to get any easier, but I hadn't decided to come home because I wanted *easy*. I wanted Mom. I'd committed to love her no matter what. And now, as I faced my first chance to show her, I realized she would be sober. God sure knew how to keep His bargains, even when He wasn't the one to make them.

Doug had to grab my elbows from behind and lift me up the stairs, because I couldn't put any weight on my feet. I stumbled through the apartment door, fell into Mom's arms, and we both sobbed. Somehow I ended up on the old couch, loving its familiar, broken springs, and Doug had my shoes and socks off. Mom sat next to me, one of my hands clasped lightly in both her bandaged ones. "Aidyn," she said. "Baby, you're OK."

All I wanted right then was to look at her, into her eyes, puffy but clear and steady; and listen to her voice, shaky and hoarse, but not slurring. Mom sober—that was all I'd ever wanted.

"Are you hungry?" Mom asked. "I've got some

soup. It's still hot. I've been waiting for you to come..." Her voice broke.

"You get it, and I'll get some medicine on these feet," Doug said. "I don't think you'll get yourself a trip to the hospital. Nothing looks infected so far, just painful."

"That's good," I told him, meaning the hospital trip.

Mom cradled two cups as she came back in. "It's easier for me to carry them this way," she said and handed both to me. "This one is cocoa."

I drank the whole cup off without stopping for breath.

Mom laughed. "I'll make some more—" But I stopped her.

"No, Mom, I just want you here. OK?"

She gave me a look, shy and delighted, and tucked her arms around her waist.

"Mom, your poor hands."

She shrugged. "I really messed myself up."

Doug came in with a first-aid kit. "I didn't tell her who's been calling."

Mom smiled. "Miguel. He called three times, baby. He's so worried. I called him as soon as we hung up, as soon as I knew you were safe. He'll come by tomorrow."

"He will? But—"

"The police found his dad. He'll have his trial, and we're all hoping he gets a good sentence. It won't be long enough, but it will give Miguel and his mother some time to figure out what they need to do next."

I closed my eyes. All the while I'd been looking for him, he'd been looking for me. Could I have done anything more stupid?

Doug finished smearing my feet with something that stung worse than the ruptured blisters had.

"Mom, I have to talk to you."

"OK." Her eyes never left my face.

Doug packed up the first-aid kit and walked back to the bathroom. He didn't come back, and I reminded myself to thank him for giving us some time alone.

"Mom, I love you."

She closed her eyes, tears spilling across her cheeks. She wiped one gauzy hand across her face. "I love you too, baby."

I pulled her hand down, holding her by the wrist so I wouldn't hurt her worse than I had to. "But I hate it when you drink."

She let out a sharp breath. "So do I."

"I won't run away again, I promise. That was really stupid. But I don't know what to do when you drink, Mom. I don't know what to do."

"I can't promise you—"

"I'm not asking you to. I just want you to try, OK? I mean, you're already trying, aren't you?"

"Yeah, I am." She lifted her chin and met my eyes. "Two days sober." She stared at her hands and sighed. "A few days ago I told everyone two months but now, all I can claim is two days."

"I know." I caught up her other hand and held them the way I'd learned from Lucy, softly, gently. The wrappings had come loose and I saw bloodstains on the inside, and red gashes laced with untidy black stitches. I tucked the gauze a little tighter, making sure not to touch her wounds. *God, I hope You're with me. I hope You help me keep my promises.*

"I guess I have to practice saying stuff like this, if I go to those meetings, you know?" I took a deep breath and blurted, "My name is Aidyn, and my mom is an alcoholic."

She bent her face to my hands, shaking hard. I lifted her chin up so I could watch her while I said, "My mom is two days sober, and I am so proud."

Thank you for purchasing this Watershed Books title.
For other inspirational stories, please visit our on-line
bookstore at www.pelicanbookgroup.com.

For questions or more information, contact us at
customer@pelicanbookgroup.com.

Watershed Books
Fiction illuminated™
an imprint of Pelican Ventures Book Group
www.PelicanBookGroup.com

May God's glory shine through
this inspirational work of fiction.

AMDG